D0658844

Arafat's Elephant

Arafat's Elephant

~: S T O R I E S :~

Jonathan Tel

COUNTERPOINT

WASHINGTON D.C.

Library of Congress Cataloging-in-Publication Data
Tel, Jonathan.
Arafat's elephant / Jonathan Tel.
p. cm.
ISBN 1-58243-183-3 (alk. paper)
1. Jerusalem—Social life and customs—Fiction.   I. Title.
PS3620.E44 A88   2002
813'.6—dc21   2001047247

Book design and composition by Mark McGarry
Set in Aldus

COUNTERPOINT
P.O. Box 65793, Washington, D.C. 20035-5793

Counterpoint is a member of the Perseus Books Group

10 9 8 7 6 5 4 3 2 1

In this land, whoever tells
the best story wins

Contents

☙ Arafat's Elephant

A Story About a Bomb

⌒ **A story about a bomb is not a bomb.** However artfully constructed the plot, however incendiary the theme, although the topic may be volatile and the implications explosive, however dangerous the sentiments may be—a story will not in fact abolish itself in a blinding flash, scattering shrapnel within a radius of forty meters and shredding passersby. Despite our best efforts.

Several years ago I browsed through an anthology of Palestinian literature. It had been lent by an Israeli acquaintance of mine (the translator, in fact, of some of my own stories) and I had to return it before leaving the country—so I am telling you about it only from memory, and with the aid of jottings in my notebook. It was one of those plump, poorly printed, catchall UNESCO jobs—comprising poetry, stories, and autobiographical fragments. As a rule, the poems did not survive translation, and the prose was highly variable in quality. There was, however, one story that struck me as remarkable at the time; and that has stayed with me since, burning in my memory. Its title was *The Red Button*.

It concerned a Hamas terrorist (or freedom fighter, if you prefer) who was on the point of blowing himself up, along with as many Israelis as possible. He was shifting from leg to leg in Jerusalem, near where the new city meets the old, across from Jaffa Gate, on the wrong side of the highway.

It was eight o'clock in the morning on the hottest Friday in August. He had come from a refugee camp in Gaza, and had spent the previous night praying with some comrades near Bethlehem. He had just been dropped off by Toyota. He was wearing a long padded overcoat, buttoned up, to conceal the bands of dynamite around his abdomen. He was sweating and shivering. His instructions were to cross the road (looking carefully to right and to left first; it wouldn't do to be knocked down by a speeding vehicle before he had a chance to press the button on the detonator) to the bus stop on the far side. With any luck, there would be many Israelis waiting there. He would simply have to stand among them, mutter *Allahu Akbar*, and the next thing he knew he would be marching into Paradise, a pair of dark-eyed houris eager to kiss his bleeding wounds. In reality, of course, it was not as simple as all that.

The stones of the city wall were solid blocks of white sun. Every bone in his body ached. (He had had to crouch on the back floor of the Toyota, concealed under a carpet, for what had seemed like generations. The car had passed through checkpoint after checkpoint, and had then been forced to idle in commuter

traffic.) He smelled his own sweat. (No, worse. His wise comrades had insisted he swallow a hefty dose of Diocalm before his
mission, to seal him up. It would hardly do to enter Paradise
stinking from one's own shit. . . . *On the Day of Resurrection*, it is
written, *the wounds of the martyr shall be perfumed like musk.*)

The bus stop in question was within view. He could see
would-be passengers waiting there, more or less patiently.
Women, children, old men, also about ten soldiers, perhaps on
weekend leave. The ideal target. Yet he had to wait. The traffic
was atrocious. He stepped into the road—and a great red Coca
Cola truck went roaring past. He retreated. He strode forth. A
Subaru blurted its horn at him. A police car swept by. He hob-
bled back to the safety of the curb. Finally the road was empty.
On the far side, a Number 23 was halted at the stop. . . . By the
time he arrived there, the bus had departed, taking all the
Israelis with it. If he reached into his pocket and jabbed down
on the button now, he would explode nobody but himself. He
could have wept with frustration.

Well, he couldn't just stand there. He was sure he looked
suspicious. He walked down Hativat Yerushalayim, as far as
where the wall bends by the Armenian Quarter. He walked up
again to Jaffa Gate. He returned to the crossing. He re-crossed
the highway. And down the street to the point where he had
begun. By now a dozen new Israelis had assembled at the bus
stop opposite. Once again he tried to cross the road. Once again
he had to reckon with the traffic. The horrible fumes. . . .

He kept the vision of Paradise clear in front of him. As it is
written: ". . . *that Allah may know those who believe, and take
martyrs from among you. . . .* " Two houris would come dancing
toward him. They would cloak him in the precious *hulla* robe.

They would say, *"May Allah put dust on the face of those who put dust on your face!"* ... An acrid aroma; a clammy feeling around the groin. He had got beyond the trembling stage. He was on an exalted level of anguish. Now the twitching was intense, as if he were being banged like a saltcellar on a humid day. There was a gap in the traffic. He darted between a taxi and a Honda motorcycle. Once again he reached the bus stop. Once again a bus, the 13 Aleph, had just accelerated away, taking his almost-victims with it.

Once again he circled down Hativat Yerushalayim and back to the beginning. Once again the frustration. Once again the shuffling at the curbside—bare feet in basic polyurethane sandals. Once again the mumbling of prayers and quotes. The agony in his guts. The unscratchable itching underneath the load of high explosives. ... And then (as anybody who knows anything about the structure of fairy tales knows) it was on the third try that the pattern was broken.

Now at last the future seemed revealed. Now a fresh selection of Israelis had appeared at the stop. Now there was a hiatus in the traffic—no vehicles to delay him, no bus to carry away his victims. And then, just as he was about to scurry across the expanse of asphalt, to leap forward into his destiny, to switch on the detonator...

A middle-aged couple approached the terrorist. They stood beside the curb, blocking his way. The man had thin sandy hair whirled over a bald spot. He was wearing baggy green shorts. An oversize map was sprouting from his shirt pocket. He was waving his yellow Holyland Tours baseball cap to attract the terrorist's attention. The woman, blonde, had on an identical cap; she was also in shorts, blue ones, matching her varicose veins. The two of them were addressing him in what he reasonably believed to be English.

Since he evidently did not understand, the tourists resorted to sign language. The man was holding up a camera—it was suspended from a strap around his neck—he was hoisting it free. The woman was pointing to it. Much dumbshow ensued, involving grasping and lifting the Olympus, gesturing at elements of it (automatic focus; you just have to aim the thing and shoot), peering through the viewfinder, and going *cheese*. . . . (And all the while, Hativat Yerushalayim remained free of traffic, the ignorant Israelis were unmoving—how simple and easy to blow them and himself up, the exemplary conclusion—if only those damn foreigners would just get out of his way!)

But what could he do? If he tried to escape from them, let alone grapple with them, he would only draw attention to himself. The Israelis would just run off, or one of them might draw a gun and kill him before he'd be able to complete his mission. No, the only hope was to go through with what the foreigners wanted, and then they would leave him in peace.

The tourists posed on the curbside. The husband put his arm around his wife's shoulder. They smiled as if they were genuinely happy. As if purely to be in Jerusalem was to be blessed. The terrorist stepped back, arranging their faces within the rectangle of the viewfinder. As a backdrop—the road. Travelers in cars, and pedestrians. An old woman, carrying a basket of oranges. Arab workmen, their pickaxes over their shoulders, en route to a building site. Soldiers waiting. Two Hassidim on bicycles, going by. Children playing hide-and-seek behind the bus shelter. And beyond that, the magnificent ancient wall of the Old City. He motioned the couple with his left hand, to lean their heads closer together; to step a little *this* way—so he could catch them with Jaffa Gate behind, for extra picturesqueness. . . . Somehow, miraculously, as he squinted through the viewfinder, all his quaverings and uncertainties had ceased. He was aware of nothing except this instant. As for the tourists, they would look at the snapshot and remember their trip to the Holy Land for the rest of their lives. . . . Ah, perfect now. The tip of an index finger pressed down on a red button—and the story ended.

ـﺑ

Of course my summary of the story doesn't capture the magic of the original. How could it? The author (a certain Ahmed Fishawi) took great pains to bring us inside the mind and body of the central character. His name is S___. We are borne along on his stream of consciousness. His thoughts focus on the here-and-now (precise physical description) along with memories and ponderings concerning his childhood in the refugee camp; his mother who is suffering from breast cancer; his elder brother who had been arrested five times during the Intifada; his uncle who had been shot in the leg at a roadblock near Gush Katzir . . . and, interspersed with that, theological reflection.

Elements of this last aspect—a discussion of the role of the martyr in a jihad—I copied into my notebook. (You will excuse any erroneous spellings, mistaken attributions, and misquotations on my part.) At the Battle of Uhud, "Abd Allah b. Jahish cried out, 'Let me meet my enemy face to face! Let him cut off my nose and ear! So that when I meet Thee, O Allah, and Thou ask of me, "For whose sake were thy nose and ear cut off?" I may answer, For Thy sake and for the sake of Thy Prophet!' "

... And did not al-Ghazzali describe martyrdom as "the most wondrous of delights"? ... A martyr, according to a tradition going back to the Prophet, "may live in any part of Paradise he choose." Also: "when the first drop of blood falls, he is granted forgiveness for all his sins." ... A martyr, alone among men, is not washed or shrouded after death, "that his bloody clothing may speak for him on the Day of Judgment." ... At the Battle of Badr, Umar b. al-Humam b. al-Jamuh al-Ansari was about to eat a date. He threw it away. "If I live to eat another date again, I shall have lived too long a life!" ... And the Prophet informed Zayd b. Suhan that part of his body would precede him into Paradise. His arm was cut off in battle; subsequently, in the Battle of the Camel, he was fatally wounded. He declared, "Lo, I see my hand in Heaven, beckoning me to follow!" ... On the other hand, suicide, generally speaking, is a horrible sin. Is it not written (Sura 2: 195): "... *and live in the way of Allah, and do not cast yourselves by your own hands into destruction*"? ... Lots more similar stuff, besides.

On first read-through, I think I was unconsciously taking in the story (printed as it was amid essays, memoirs, and confessional poems) as if it were factual—a window into the experience of Palestinians. And so I was moved. ... The second time I read it, I became aware of the technical expertise of the author. ... And the third time, I was disturbed.

What exactly was the author, this Mr. Fishawi, trying to say? Was he drawing an analogy between terrorist and tourist? Just as the former regards innocent victims as items that serve a function in a theologico-political calculation—so the latter sees Jerusalem, complete with inhabitants, merely as a setting for a holiday. Each, in his or her own way, is an exploiter. ... But this is absurd! It's one thing to put outsiders in an album, quite another to rip them apart.

Furthermore, as the years have gone by, as this story has lived on in my head, I have come to wonder. Perhaps the author was *too* good a writer. He has taken us *too* much inside the mind of a terrorist. Of course that is the author's job. (A fiction writer can go places no journalist could ever venture.) But if we are brought to—more than understand—to *sympathize* with the terrorist, then are we not, in some sense, colluding with him? Far be it from me to criticize another author on these grounds, let alone call for censorship. I only wish to draw attention to my feelings of discomfort. The grander questions I leave open.

Naturally, over the years, whenever I have encountered Arab intellectuals, I have mentioned this story. None of them had read *The Red Button*, or had heard of Ahmed Fishawi. Well that's how it is on occasion; it happens that an individual—who normally never writes fiction at all, or badly—will pen one, luminous story (as a rule, deriving from his own experience). Nothing he had ever done before or will ever do again is re-motely comparable. I thought of contacting my Hebrew translator and getting him to fax me a copy, so I could show it around to friends and colleagues and associates; but in truth I wasn't at all sure I ever wanted to deal with the story again.

Until—the other day—I was at a party in Tel Aviv. It was taking place in a penthouse suite at the top of what, by local standards, qualifies as a skyscraper. The apartment belonged to a children's book illustrator (heiress to a real estate fortune, hence the setting) and her husband, a writer of techno-thrillers.

The guests were mostly connected to the world of books—poets, journalists, a scattering of fictioneers. I had been brought here by my Israeli publisher. The view was amazing—a night-time panorama of the city, and the Mediterranean beyond. The air conditioning was intense. (We had been warned not to open the windows, lest a gull swoop in and snatch a slice of goat-cheese focaccia from our fingers. "Greedy bastards!" the techno-thriller author had remarked.)

As usual in Israel, the guests were arguing about politics. I say "arguing"—for certainly voices were raised, fists were being shaken, everybody was fiercely interrupting everybody else—yet, as far as I could tell, the guests were pretty much in agreement. We all were in favor of peace, were we not; normalization; human rights; an equitable settlement with the Palestinians? Now, happy as I was to sip my gracious host and hostess's Tishbi cabernet sauvignon, to listen in on these good people reciting draft versions of editorials to be appearing soon enough in the peacenik Israeli press, I did yearn for meatier conversation. . . . I noticed a man standing by himself to one side, saying nothing. His hands were opening and shutting like lobster claws. He had buttoned himself into a tan summer suit, which he did not seem to belong in, as if handed down from an elder brother. His short black hair did not so much sprout from his skull as cling to it, like a colony of barnacles; sunglasses were growing on top of his head.

I managed to trap him between a floor lamp and a high glass tabletop. A bookcase was at my side; on top of it a white china bowl brimful with pomegranates. I introduced myself. "What do you think of all this?" I asked him.

He stuffed a strip of pita dunked in taramosalata in his

mouth, and washed it down with Kinley soda—thus avoiding having to respond.

I asked next, "What's your connection with this party?"

He made a dismissive gesture with a bowl of guacamole.

But eventually, when he was satisfied nobody was overhearing our conversation, he loosened up.

"Fucking liberal losers," he said. "What do they know? The only Arabs they ever see are the guys who pick up their garbage. Believe you me, ninety-nine percent of the Palestinians support Hamas—whether they admit it or not. The only way we'll have peace is if the Arabs know there's a gun pointing at their head."

"That's an interesting point of view," I said. "Can you pass the pistachios?"

"Sure."

"What kind of writing do you do?"

He seemed startled by my question. "I use an IBM-compatible laptop. How about you?"

I think we talked about computers, and food and drink, and the weather for a while. . . .

And then, since we were fast running out of conversational topics, I alluded to *The Red Button*.

To my surprise, the man gave a broad grin.

"I know that piece. Yes, J___. I know it very well."

"Really? Where did you come across it?"

"I didn't have to 'come across it.' The author's a good friend of mine. We go back a long way."

"You know Ahmed Fishawi?"

"Of course. But it's not his real name. It's his" (in an atrocious French accent) "*nom de plume . . . nom de guerre. . . .*"

He refilled his own glass with Kinley, and mine with Tishbi.

I murmured some literary criticism of a conventional sort, praising the author's talent in drawing us into his fictional world.

The man ignored me. He raised his glass as if about to deliver a toast.

"As a matter of fact—I am Ahmed Fishawi."

Since—in my astonishment—I had not raised my glass, he "clinked" his against empty air. "*L'Chaim!*" Then he swigged the glass of soda in one gulp.

He added, "And by the way, don't keep calling it 'fiction.' Fiction shmiction! *The Red Button* is true, every word of it. The events described took place on the morning of August 8th, 1999. I know because I was there."

"You're Ahmed Fishawi?" I said, stunned.

"That's what I keep telling you."

"Now wait a minute," I said. "I can just about believe that you wrote the story, and published it under a pseudonym in an anthology of Palestinian literature. But you are not seriously telling me that you personally are a Palestinian terrorist! . . . So what other character could you have been? I know you're not a foreign tourist with a camera. And even if you had been waiting at the bus stop, you wouldn't have known what was going on."

"All the same," he said, "I was there. . . . Do you believe everything you read in books, J___? Do you believe it's not just the truth, but the whole truth? I was there all along, standing just out of frame. . . . And the real story goes on, after the story on the page ends. Do you want to know what actually happened? Or are you one of those post-fucking-modernists?"

"I want to know the truth."

"I was there. I was leaning against a lamppost, fascinated by the sports pages in *Ma'ariv*. On the other side of the terrorist, a couple of lovers were kissing. . . . So the terrorist pressed the red button on the camera. . . . At that moment—when we knew for sure he wouldn't have a free hand to operate the detonator—I came running up from behind and I slammed into his back. The 'lovers' seized his arms between them. And the male 'tourist' put on the handcuffs while the female 'tourist' kicked him in the balls."

The man laughed.

"My real name's E___. I'm in counter-terrorism—Shimshon Unit. Have you heard of us? We'd been following the poor bastard ever since he left Gaza. We eliminated his entire cell."

The man laughed louder. His shoulder knocked against the floor lamp, and set it vibrating, its bulb flashing on and off.

"I almost killed myself! And everybody else too! You know that? See, when I ran into him, somehow the detonator started up. It shouldn't have—maybe it was a faulty electrical connection, I don't know. By a miracle it didn't set the bomb off. So all that happened was that the bastard got third degree burns on his belly, and I screwed up my arm."

He rolled up his right sleeve. Just above the wrist, a patch of skin was distorted, thickly ridged—as if the flesh had melted like wax and refrozen.

I took the opportunity to tell him my full name, and what I was doing in Israel.

"Yes yes," he said with a show of uninterest. "I know all about you."

He stared past my shoulder.

"So then we took him back to HQ. We put him in the medical unit for a while—Intensive Care—until we knew he wasn't going to die on us, and he was out of pain. Then we could torture him. Don't look so shocked, J___. We call it torture but it's not what you think of as torture, it's the gentle art of persuasion. We're not in Argentina, you know. We use the official methods. *Shabah*—making him sit in one position for hours, in a child-size chair. *Tiltulim*—shaking him till he rattles. Those softies over there...," pointing with an asparagus tip at a group of giggling novelists, "they think I'm naughty—but it's toughies like me who stop the Arabs blowing up the kindergartens!"

He made himself a rough-and-ready sandwich of cherry tomatoes, asparagus tips and baba ganoush, wrapped in pita bread, and lowered it into his mouth. When he had chewed most of it, he went on.

"Of course we didn't have to torture him, hardly at all. Not in his case. He knew he'd be spending years in an Israeli prison, instead of partying with houris in Paradise. He didn't want to be alive. We stood beside the hospital bed, and we shouted at him. So he told us the names and addresses. Everything we wanted to know. Most of it we knew already, actually. Who his commander was, the location of his safe house. The basic facts.... Not that we can do fuck-all about it, if it's in the Palestinian Authority area.... And then we locked him up, and that was the end of that."

I was silent.

I wondered if he was trying to fool me, or fooling himself as well.

The man reached past me and took a pomegranate. He bit it

open. He started sucking its juice, and spitting pith and seeds onto the carpet, as if daring me to challenge him.

I tried to respond indirectly.

"I think you underestimate yourself," I said. "You say you're not a fiction writer—and maybe the outline of your story is based on truth—but how on earth did you get inside the man's head? Those interior monologues. I can't believe this is your first story!"

"Oh I've published a few children's books. . . . This is my first adult fiction—and I'm not going to do another, ever again. It's hard work."

He pulled down his sunglasses, blocking out his eyes.

"I asked the bastard to help me. That's how I know. Not too bad a fellow, the terrorist, once you get to be friends with him. I gave him a Marlboro. I played the nice guy. I said, if you tell me every little thing that went through your head, I'll let you read the Quran, and I'll give you the cutest little prayer mat to keep you company. . . . And then when he'd told me everything he could think of, I used the other method to jog his memory."

"What other method?" I said.

I literally felt the hairs stand up on my neck—a sensation I'd only ever read about in books, that I'd always supposed to be fictional. An excitement like that a hunter feels, I imagine, when the object of the chase is within sight; or like that of a writer who has at last found a way to construct his narrative, uniting form and content.

"What method do you think?" he said. "The usual. What a man like you would call background research. I went down to his cell and I tied a blanket soaked in piss over his head. Then I patted him in the kidneys with the butt of my rifle. . . . It took seventy-two hours before he broke. He answered all my questions."

I took a pack of Winstons from my pocket, shook it out, and offered him one.

He ignored my offer.

"I don't need to tell *you* what he said. Every little detail, and more besides. His childhood. His grandmother. His uncle. His religious beliefs. What he felt and what he smelled. And it was worth it. A chance in a lifetime.... *The Red Button*'s a great story, you told me so yourself...."

Then, suddenly, without warning, he charged past, pushing me out of his way.

He had vanished.

I gazed through the picture window. Stars, part of a moon; city lights diffusing eerily into photochemical smog; searchlights over the Mediterranean, destroyers on the horizon.... Somewhere behind me, my Israeli publisher and my American publisher were murmuring lovingly together; elsewhere, poets were swapping malicious gossip: loud whispers in ferocious Hebrew.... It was chilly. My hands were plunged in my pockets. Meanwhile I let my thoughts roam back again and again, analyzing and questioning the version in the book, and his version....

I was jolted from my reverie by a voice, close to my left ear:

"I've given it up. A bad habit. Don't mind if you do."

I looked straight at E___. I saw fractions of myself mirrored in his sunglasses.

He shrugged.

"So what are you going to do now, J___? Are you going to put me in one of your stories—me along with S___? . . . It's up to you. I can't stop you. It's *your* story now."

Ibrahim Kuttab Is Innocent

"But I don't understand," I said. "How could a man like him do a thing like that?"

"Well maybe if you'd listen for a change instead of interrupting me the whole time—you and your fantastic stories!—maybe you'd actually find out what happened."

"Okay, then. So what was his real name?"

"Avraham Krivitsky."

"Kuvitsky?"

"No. *Kri*vitsky. Rhymes with 'criminal.'"

"And where was he born?"

"Like I told you, Rishon-le-Zion. He grew up in a respectable middle-class family. Nothing remarkable. Just your regular, Gimel-average high school dropout. If he'd had the common sense to keep his head down and play along with the system, nothing would have happened to him, and we wouldn't be having this conversation."

"But he pretended to be an—!"

"Listen! How many times do I have to tell you? Who's telling this story, me or you?"

"Sorry. I'll keep quiet from now on."

"I should hope so. So... where was I, before you interrupted me?... Oh yes. Avraham Krivitsky. The Jew who pretended he was an Arab. Why? Why do you think? Because he had a profound respect for Arab culture? Because this voice spoke to him telling him to convert to Islam? There's only one reason why any idiot of a seventeen-year-old should try to pass himself off as an Arab. Because he wanted to dodge his military service, of course!"

"And did it work?"

"Kind of. Not really. Yes and no. You've got to understand how the bureaucracy functions. He was called up, so he sends them a letter saying it's all a mistake, he's really an Israeli Arab, and as such he isn't liable for the draft. And they send him back a letter saying he's got to appear before them on such-and-such a day. So along he goes—this kid speaking fluent Hebrew telling them he's an Arab, and he shows them an ID in the name of Ibrahim Kuttab, and naturally they don't believe him but they don't have the authority to make a decision there and then—so they tell him to come back a week later, with more proof."

"So does he?"

"No. They never see him again."

"And the ID?"

"You can get them on the black market. It's no big deal."

"So what did he do next?"

"Left home, moved to Nahariya, and got a job. Lots of jobs. The kind of job you can get if you're an Arab and you're not too picky. Some laboring—but he didn't have the muscles for that, and anyway there's all the competition from the Romanians and the Turks and even Ghanaians nowadays. Mostly, he washed dishes in hummus places; did the shit work in a pizzeria—that kind of thing. He told them he was an illegal from the Territories. Payment strictly under the table."

"And did he speak Arabic?"

"Are you joking? No more than you and me. Of course he knows the words everybody knows—*shawarma!*—*halva!*—*shabab!*—*intifada!*—and all those rude words your *Ima* doesn't know you know. He spoke to his bosses in broken Hebrew—they don't care. . . . They say he was a pretty good worker."

"And did he look like an Arab?"

"Avraham? No way! He had light brown hair, blue eyes. . . . Of course, some Palestinians do look like that, it's true. If anybody asked, he'd tell them he had Circassian ancestors, who had come here during the Ottoman Empire—or sometimes he said his eyes came from the Crusades. But as a matter of fact, you know, most employers don't indulge in chit-chat with their illegals. . . . The truth is, we take people for what they say they are. I mean, just like you told me, who in their right mind is going to say they're an Arab when they're not?"

"But what about his fellow Arabs? The people he worked alongside? Didn't they suspect?"

"Now that's a good question. I don't exactly know about this—but I can think of two alternatives; maybe three. Number

One. Maybe he always worked on his own? One thing we do know about Avraham, he was definitely your classic loner. Number Two. Maybe he spoke to the Arabs in broken Hebrew, and gave some bullshit excuse about not wanting to talk Arabic in front of the boss. . . . Okay, I guess this doesn't sound very likely . . . I'm just trying to not rule out possibilities."

"And Number Three?"

"What?"

"You said there was a third explanation."

"Really? Now what could that be? Well maybe . . . maybe the Arabs knew all along he was a faker, but they thought it was a good joke—or they thought he was crazy—whatever. . . ."

"He *was* crazy."

"Yes. . . . So Avraham's working in a butcher's in Nahariya—he's been there for like a month—sweeping the floor, cleaning the counter, that kind of thing. And one day the place gets raided. There's a security alert. Some bomb hoax deal. Anyway, the cops swarm all down the street, and of course they arrest anybody with an Arab ID. . . . They take him to the police station. They get this Druse interrogator who fires questions at him in fluent Arabic—and when he doesn't answer, they just assume he's being naughty. They throw him in a cell, and they beat him up a little. And the following morning the ID check has gone through. They've worked out he's not really Ibrahim Kuttab—they can tell a fake ID when they see one—but they don't know who he really is. They beat him up a little more. But he still won't break. Finally they put two and two together—he looks like a Jew—he apparently can't speak Arabic—they do a crosscheck with the missing persons list, and they've got a pretty shrewd idea they're speaking to Avraham Krivitsky."

"So does he confess then?"

"You'd think so, wouldn't you? I mean, the worst that can happen to him is he gets busted for dodging his service. What with his behavior he's pretty much guaranteed a psychiatric exemption now—not to mention an exemption on the grounds of being a criminal and general weirdo—so he'd just have to spend three months in jail, max . . . and then he can go back to pretending to be an Arab. He can pretend to be Osama Bin Laden, if it makes him happy."

"So his family—"

"Hey! I'm the one telling this story. Remember? His family, sure. They haven't seen him for over a year. He hasn't really got much of a family—his parents are divorced—his *Abba* lives in Tel Aviv, with his kid step-sister. . . . His *Ima*, she gets driven in from Rishon-le-Zion. And she looks at her precious little Avraham, he's in a jail cell, unshaven, bruised, and she bursts into tears and she tries to hug him through the bars, *Avi! I love you so much! How could they ever do this to you?* Blah, blah, blah."

"Poor woman."

"Hmm. And—now this is the weirdest—he still doesn't admit who he is! The police know who he is. His own mother is standing right there, weeping all over her shoes. And he just yammers away in broken Arabish-Hebrew. *Me is Ibrahim Kuttab.*"

"And his mother?"

"Never mind his mother! Think about him! The clown! The cops want to kick him out—they have enough to do taking care of real criminals—but of course they can't, because he's wanted on a charge now. . . . So they send a fax to the military police telling them to take the bastard away—and they fax back saying they're busy, they'll pick him up tomorrow."

"So nobody wants him."

"Avraham's locked up in solitary overnight—and when they check his cell in the morning, he's put his belt around his neck, he's hanged himself, and he's left a suicide note written in his own blood on the wall, in Hebrew of course, *I AM INNOCENT*, and it's signed *IBRAHIM KUTTAB*."

"What a sad story."

"Yes."

"Why did he do it?"

"Who knows?"

"What does it mean?"

"You tell me."

"How did you hear about it?"

"Me?"

"Yes. You."

"Well I—"

"Was it in the papers?"

"What? No. This kind of story, it's not the kind of thing they print. I mean, who benefits? The army? The police? The family, now they don't want everybody to know that their son. . . . No, it wasn't in the papers."

"So you heard about it through friends?"

"What friends? Do you think I have friends in jail? Do you think I have the kind of friends who spend their free time in police stations, picking up gossip?"

"I was just wondering—"

"Stop wondering."

"Was it through your own military service then?"

"Me? My service?"

"Well, you've told me a lot of stories, all about interesting things that happened to you when you were in the army, and about people you met and the stories *they* told you, and even the stories that people had told people and *those* people told you—or maybe I'm thinking it wasn't your actual *service* but during your *reserve* duty . . . so I naturally assumed. . . ."

"If you really want to know the answer, you have to let me complete the story."

"I thought it *was* finished. The man's dead. What else can happen to him?"

"Not him. The *other* Ibrahim Kuttab."

"There's another? There's more than one Jew pretending he's an Arab called Ibrahim Kuttab!?"

"How many do you want? No—there's just one Jew in this story, and just one Arab. The Arab is the *real* Ibrahim Kuttab. . . . When the cops found out Avraham was using a fake ID, they traced where his ID had come from. . . . Let's have a big hand for—Mr. Ibrahim Kuttab! Born and bred in Umm al-Fahm. Age 24. A carpenter, married, with two kids . . . The border police reckoned there was a security issue—so the Shin Bet got involved."

"No fun for Ibrahim."

"Absolutely not. He got beaten up in turn. They tied him to a chair, blindfolded him, and hit him with rifle butts. Finally they believed him when he said he had nothing to do with it. His ID had been stolen a couple of years earlier. He'd reported it to the authorities, and he had a replacement. Obviously, whoever had stolen it had altered the photo, doctored it, and passed it on to Avraham."

"Just Ibrahim's unlucky day."

"Just everybody's unlucky day."

"So—wait a minute—I'm not sure I'm getting this. Ibrahim. The real one. What did he do? Did he pass himself off as a Jew? Did he pretend he was Avraham?"

"Have you been listening to a word I've been saying! Have you been sitting here with your fingers in your ears! I swear, you deliberately misunderstand my stories, because you think you can "improve" them and write them down and pretend they're your own.... Now you'd better listen carefully because I'm not going to repeat this a second time. IBRAHIM KUTTAB IS INNOCENT! HE IS WHO HE SAYS HE IS! HE HAS NOTHING TO DO WITH ANY DECEPTION!"

"Okay, I think I heard that."

"Throughout the entire story you have just heard, Ibrahim Kuttab was minding his own business. He was making love to his wife. He was cuddling his eldest son. He was celebrating the birth of his daughter. He was conceiving his next child, who is on the way. He was ... well, what is it carpenters do all day long? ... cutting wood, sanding it, measuring it with a ruler—"

"Hey, you still haven't told me how you got to hear about all this."

"I was coming to that. Now listen, my grandfather passed away last March."

"I'm sorry."

"Don't be. He was eighty-four. He'd been ill a long time. Kidney disease. A blessing, in its way.... So I happened to be in Nahariyah a couple of Tuesdays ago, on business, and that's where my grandfather, my *Saba*, where he's buried. So I thought I'd go along to the cemetery, and pay my respects."

"Very decent of you."

"And I'm in the cemetery, saying a little prayer—not that I believe, but I know *Saba*'d like that—piling pebbles on his grave the way you're supposed to, it's the thought that counts. And over at the next grave, a man is kneeling and swaying. . . ."

"And that grave is the grave of—"

"Yes. It's where Avraham Krivitsky is buried. It's the anniversary of his death."

"And the mourner is his brother?"

"What brother? He doesn't have a brother."

"His father then?"

"No. His family have cut him off. They want nothing to do with him. He disgraced them, even in death."

"So the man by the grave . . . "

"The man by the grave. He's swarthy. He's wearing plastic sandals. He's got a red-checked keffiyah around his head. He's weeping his heart out. . . . Ibrahim Kuttab was mourning the death and life of the other Ibrahim Kuttab. He told me everything."

Beautiful, Strong, and Modest

꙳ A dozen stray cats were munching nobbly red objects and Dinah was walking down Jaffa Road on the way to meet the man who would become her husband probably and when she drew closer she recognized them as roosters' heads. Well what else is there to do with the heads after the poor creatures have had their necks chopped? she thought. You only need one male for an entire barnyard of females; funny if it were the same with humans. The heads were in an open cardboard box. They say that headless chickens can go for quite long trips before they die. Cat upon cat arrived sneaking in from all over Jerusalem; there must have been at least twenty of them gnawing the combs and quarreling over the remains. Dinah wasn't at all sure this was a proper subject for her to be blinking short-sightedly at but she had already seen all she was capable of seeing—too late to worry about it now.

She had recently come in at the Central Bus Station on the direct line from the suburb of Modi'in, where she lived. In less than an hour she should be in the lobby of the King Hezekiah Hotel, which was on the far side of town. All the same she might as well keep on going by foot—it's not as if her prospective fiancé would escape.

Under the February sun parts of her were too hot and parts were too cold; she didn't let this bother her. Naturally she was wearing denser, more enveloping clothes than usual—you can never be too prim on such occasions. Plain black shoes, an ankle-length black skirt, a white blouse and a black jacket. Anyway black suited her complexion. Now and again she bit her lips, to redden them—she was aiming at the Snow White look. Her panty hose was what she was fondest of: it was practically brand new, a cotton–Lycra mix that didn't sag at all and had been specially imported from Flatbush, New York, in a package that described itself (in Yiddish and Hebrew) as *A Revolution In Legwear! Beautiful, Strong, and Modest!* Of course it was the thickest kind—denier 70. There had been much discussion at the makhon she attended concerning the appropriate denier for a nice Jewish girl (Rabbi Pinter was quite forceful on the subject)—so much so in fact that Dinah suspected "denier" was a Yiddish word.

Also there had been an English label on the panty hose. She had assumed it said the same as the Hebrew, though she wasn't really sure. Well it wasn't likely to claim the opposite—*Ugly, Weak, and Shameless!* Such a peculiar language—the letters all run the wrong way and the spelling is madness. . . .

With the flat of her hand she smoothed her hair. When she would be married, it would all have to go, snipped till it was shorter than a man's. She imagined laying her head on a block, and a big axe falling. Then she would have only stubble; how different it would feel.

A colorful mist was drifting toward her along the road, which condensed into a group of foreign tourists, boys and girls about her own age. She passed through them without contact. They were dressed in what looked to her like underclothes. Several arms were goosebumped. Dinah wished she had brought her glasses; it was only vanity that had prevented her—well, she never claimed to be perfect. A girl had her arm around a boy—whom she was unlikely to be even thinking of getting married to. How confusing. On the whole Dinah was glad she wouldn't have to be dealing with such complications, personally.

This would-be husband of hers . . . his name was Yitzhok. Now, Yitzhok's study-partner's cousin was Dinah's best friend at the makhon, Leah—and according to her, the fellow was slim with gray eyes and curly hair, and he laughed a lot, and he was an ace at basketball. Well that was fair enough. You had to have a husband after all, and unless he turned out to be a complete schmuck, she would accept him.

This was how it would be. She would appear in the lobby, and he would already be there. (It's best for the girl to be a few minutes late, so she doesn't have to wait around on her own.) He would have been given her description. "Sholem aleichem, Dinah," he'd say, by way of formal greeting; then it would be her turn: "Aleichem sholem, Yitzhok." They'd take their seats in what she imagined as high thrones, stiff and narrow, on opposite sides of a massive table, and they'd have a conver-sation about the weather or the traffic, and order drinks (for her, Coca Cola), and then ... what do people do next? ... Oh, schmooze about family and studies, who they know in common. ... Of course there were some girls in Dinah's class whose parents wouldn't permit them to meet a would-be husband unchaperoned, not even for a few minutes in a public space; but that was overdoing it: there have to be limits, even to modesty.

Dinah noticed a religious young man striding down Jaffa Road. He was stepping out into the gutter, overtaking a crowd of tourists and shoppers; he accelerated past. He fitted the description of Yitzhok well enough. Might he possibly be ... ? She was tempted to run up behind, slap her hands over the stranger's eyes, and whisper, "Guess who?" ... And the funny thing is, at any given moment in the lobby of the Hezekiah, there are often several religious couples going through the same ritual of introduction. She wondered if people ever make mistakes (after all there are only so many names; for example, Dinah and Yitzhok are common enough) and end up becoming engaged to the wrong partner!

Actually she'd been told he'd be carrying a blue book. But that wasn't much of a clue. She imagined a giant book, sky-blue—the kind a recording angel might use. ... In reality it was likely to be small and squat, dark blue, some learned commentary.

Her route took her into Zion Square and beyond, a stone's throw from a major department store. And it occurred to her she needed something extra. A nice new scarf. Not that her neck wasn't decent (no collarbone visible), but this Yitzhok might be a stickler. Also, to be honest, she always enjoyed shopping. Not that she was materialistic, but she found that shopping calmed and reassured her; it kept her in touch with the world of things. . . . Simple, plain, but in a high-quality fabric, caressable . . . She glanced at her watch. Half an hour to go.

Soon enough Dinah had found the scarf section, and had chosen one in black (safest; and it goes with everything) made from the finest silk, so thin it would fit through an engagement ring. She paid for it, using her Isracard; she signed on the dotted line. (Expensive, for what it is: but it's not as if she were contemplating an entire outfit of translucent black silk.) And she headed for the exit.

Just then, however, an alarm went off. A kind of loud buzzer, really. At first she didn't associate it with herself. Just one of the many distractions (a delivery van backing up; somebody's beeper; a bomb alert) that urban life is made up of. Then the security guard—a tiny knitted kipa perched on top of a big tanned head—said, "Lady, you need to go back."

"You think so?"

"You're tagged, Lady."

"In truth?"

"Your security tag. It's still on you. You have to go back to the checkout."

And then, taking into account what he interpreted as a fearful look, he added, "Don't worry, Lady. It happens all the time."

So Dinah returned and, after a brief discussion with the Russian cashier, had the tag on her scarf deactivated and detached. And she passed through the barrier again, this time in silence.

However, just as she was on the point of leaving the department store, a head-shawl with a floral pattern, swarthy skin, a middle-aged woman who was by her accent a Yemenite, slid up beside Dinah and hissed in her ear, *"You were shamed."*

"What?"

"I saw the whole thing," the Yemenite said. "They shamed you. You must go to the manager, and tell him what happened. He will give you a present."

"Why should I get a present?"

And the Yemenite woman, as if explaining to a little girl, repeated, *"Because you were shamed!"*

Now Dinah was in two minds. True, it would be pleasant to receive a little something: that couldn't be denied. But she was in no position to waste time; she was well behind schedule (though at a pinch she could always dial through on her Pelephone to her parents who would dial his parents who would dial him—in the modern world, nobody's completely out of reach). Besides, she wasn't at all sure she was entitled. . . .

"Where's the manager?" she asked the security guard.

And she was given directions to go upstairs and follow the signs.

She found herself in front of a receptionist.

"What do you want?"

"I'm looking for the manager, please."

"The who?"

"The manager."

"He's not here."

"When will he be back?"

"How should I know?"

Dinah sat down on a convenient packing crate. She relaxed her eyes, letting the world become a restful blur.

She took the silk scarf out of its bag, and stretched it between her hands, making it into a rope, as if about to tie up something or someone. Then she swished it loosely around her

own neck. It swung into position, and the tail flopped up farther, reaching the nape. Next she tried it out in front of her
eyes as a kind of blindfold. It was interesting how it could be
almost transparent and totally opaque, depending on how she
folded it.

She spent the subsequent—how long? ten minutes? half an
hour?—playing with the scarf.

Meanwhile, the receptionist, relenting, had been on the
switchboard to the manager.

"Okay. He's in his office now."

Dinah did not look up.

"You want to see the manager or don't you?"

Strictly speaking, she shouldn't even be thinking about
going into a man's office without a chaperone.

"He will give me my present," she informed the receptionist as she went down the uncarpeted passageway and into the
manager's office.

A minute later, she had narrated her story.

The manager, a man all hands and feet, had been writhing
on the swivel chair while she'd been speaking. He grunted. "So?
What do you want me to do about it?"

"You should compensate me."

The manager jabbed his thumb in the air. "You want compensation. And why?"

"Because—"

Interrupting:

"Was the security guard rude to you?"

"Oh, no. He was very polite."

"And the checkout girl. Was she rude?"

"No, no."

"So everything is fine. Bye-bye."

The manager shuffled some papers on his desk, and pretended to be unaware of her existence. He crossed his legs—just one of the many queer things that secular people do. Dinah wondered if it hurt.

"But it was unpleasant."

"So? Unpleasant things happen all the time. They happen to me, a hundred a day, believe you me."

"No, you don't understand. *I was shamed.*"

The manager nodded slowly. He stood up and looked Dinah in the eye. Without shifting his gaze, he pulled open a drawer in his desk—which turned out to be filled with identical rectangular packages in candy-striped wrapping paper.

And now Dinah understood what the security guard and the Yemenite had been trying to communicate. This must happen often. A lot of women and girls are shamed by the department store on a regular basis. And this is their reward.

She accepted the offering and left the store.

Outside, on a bench in Zion Square, she set about exposing the object. She tore the outer paper off with her nails. And a cellophane layer within, she clawed that off too. And inside that, cardboard. And inside that, finally, a plastic tube—white with gold lettering—a kind of cosmetics, the Ahava ("Love") brand.

Dinah held the label a centimeter from her eyeballs.

Ahava Face Pack. Rejuvenating Mud made from Genuine Dead Sea Extracts. Contains Twelve Essential Minerals.

Dinah kept on reading, taking in all the descriptions and ingredients and small print in Hebrew, and then she did her best with the English translation. If she was to believe the claims, this product, once applied to her face, was liable to take decades off her appearance. . . . Of course, if it took off so much as a single decade, she would look seven years old—she couldn't imagine Yitzhok would approve. . . .

Just then her cellular phone rang.

To be precise, it seemed to be her handbag that was ringing. That it was the phone within which was responsible for the noise could not be taken for granted.

"Maybe they forgot to deactivate the tag?" she wondered.

Eventually she clicked open the handbag and held it up to her ear patiently for several seconds. Should she answer or not? Just as she was about to pick up the phone, the noise ceased.

She dropped the Ahava inside, and snapped the bag shut.

She was aware her response might not have been wholly logical; but she felt, under the circumstances, nobody could have expected more of her.

Anyway, this counted as a signal: she should hurry along to the Hezekiah. She checked her watch. She was nearly an hour late. . . . So late, surely, there seemed no point in frittering away money on a taxi. She would stroll at a comfortable pace.

She continued along Jaffa Road until the turning to Queen Shlomzion Street, and then along that (she saw a yellowish fog which she knew was actually a vista of the walls of the Old City) to where five roads meet. . . . None of the passersby— religious Jews and secular Jews, Arabs and foreigners—paid her any particular attention, and she rejoiced in her own inconspicuousness. Only she knew the secret within her handbag.

While she was coming down Keren HaYesod Street, the ringing started up again. Having not answered earlier, there didn't seem much point in doing so at this stage. Besides, there was no proof: there are said to be people who hear ringing in their ears permanently. Dinah wondered what that might be like.

The sun was low, now. It was becoming cool. She shivered. . . . She let herself shiver some more. . . .

The King Hezekiah Hotel.

A doorman with a drooping eyelid seemed to wink at Dinah for a second; identified her type; then turned away.

The plate-glass doors glided apart automatically.

She sat down not too far from the entrance on a broad off-white armchair, covered in a plastic material intended to resemble leather, and stuffed with some substance that seeks to absorb the sitter's buttocks. A table, rather too low to be practical, a stool almost, was in front of her.

She rubbed her eyelids.

She was so convinced she knew what was coming next in her life, that she could almost hear the words. *"Sholem aleichem, so you must be Dinah?"*—but in this world no voice spoke to her.

Eventually she peered around.

She noted two, possibly three, other couples, here for the same purpose as herself. They were sitting very upright. Now and again a remark was audible. *". . . I have seven sisters . . . My study-partner is Mrs. Baruch's grandson . . . If God wills . . . My third brother has a qualification in bookkeeping. . . ."*

She wondered if a blue book was hiding somewhere. Sky-blue, a vast oblong—or a quadrilateral patch of it. Actually any-

thing would do, any shade of palish blue, any size or shape. . . .
And in the whole lobby, there was nothing. . . . It was only
when she looked over her shoulder and through the glass doors
that she saw, outside, in the space above the rooftops, a scrap of
red sky and Dinah realized she was in the wrong place at the
wrong time.

She closed her eyes. When she opened them, a smiling man
was seated in the chair opposite her. However he was unlikely
to be Yitzhok, given that he was in his forties, was wearing a
tweed suit, and had colorless eyes and short blond hair with no
head-covering. He was drinking something yellow. It didn't
really match his hair.

"Cheers!" he said in English, raising his glass.

Dinah wondered if she were dreaming, or suffering from
amnesia, or if he was. Had this Anglo-Saxon come all the way
to the King Hezekiah Hotel in Jerusalem to seek a wife?

"I'm here on business," he stated. "Import-export's my line."

Dinah wondered what country he came from. England?
America? . . . She didn't think she'd be able to cope. Her English
wasn't up to complex interactions. . . . Australia? Canada? . . .
But she'd do her best. She'd leap over the language gap, if she
could. There was an oral exercise she'd been given ten out of
ten for: *Excuse me, sir. I am lost. Can you tell me the way to
Buckingham Palace?*

"What are you having?" he asked genially.

She felt a little proud that she knew the answer to this one.

"Coca Cola," she confessed.

And she added, since it seemed only polite, "I'm Dinah."

"My pleasure, Diana," said the stranger. And he snapped his
fingers for the waiter.

When the drink came, he poured some of his own into her Coca Cola. Strangely, the fluid, so yellow in the glass, seemed transparent when it passed through the air into hers.

She muttered the general-purpose blessing—*"Blessed are You, Adonai, God, Ruler of the Universe, for Everything Lives by Your Word"*—and sipped. She supposed the kind of secular girl who would be called Diana would think nothing of sharing drinks with foreigners in hotel lobbies. She was in no position to object.

The Coke tasted not abnormal.

Something was butting against her ankles. At first she thought it was a leg of the table, and then she wondered if it might be the hotel cat, or even the hotel rat; she didn't dare peek. And by the time she'd worked out it was the Anglo-Saxon's foot, it seemed too late to do much about it. Possibly ankle-nudging was a traditional Anglo-Saxon custom—one of the many things they don't teach you in the makhon. Once, some of the girls had passed around under the desks a copy of *National Geographic:* it had contained a picture of a young man in New Guinea who was wearing nothing except stripes of body paint and a kind of sheath made from leaves. Comparatively speaking, she could scarcely object to having her shin rubbed against by a foreigner's shoe.

"Do you come here often, Diana?"

"No. Yes. I'm from here."

"Really? From here? You are here all the time?"

"I never leave."

He laughed. Which was surely to the good. If their conversation was supposed to be a joke, then it probably didn't matter that she couldn't make sense of it. He kept on laughing. She wondered if he might be drunk. Her own father and brothers got drunk only once a year, on Purim, as a religious obligation; she was trying to recall if they laughed a lot then.

There was money in her handbag. Searching for it gave her an opportunity to tuck her feet under the chair. She put the payment for her drink up on the table. But—"Allow me"—now the Anglo-Saxon's hand was covering hers. A gold wedding band was on his fourth finger. Very peculiar. She was sure Rabbi Pinter would not approve. Yet she did not move her hand . . . she was already shamed, after all. . . . And as the businessman guided her away beyond the lobby into a high echoing atrium and then toward an elevator, she still did not protest or resist.

The interior walls of the elevator were mirrored. Multiple reflections—executive with teenager, Anglo-Saxon with Israeli, male with female, goy with Jew—chaperoned Dinah. Which was reassuring, in its way. No doubt everything that happens to one person in one place once, happens to many, in many, many times over. . . .

Some seconds later, a bedroom ceiling was spinning—but she didn't see that it could be her fault.

"I have to put on my glasses," she said weakly. She stroked the pillow behind her head, and sunk her hand into the depths of her hair, as if she might have left something there.

Her gaze defocused. Nevertheless parts of the foreigner remained quite clear.

"How do I convert?" Dinah asked silently. *"How do I convert to Anglo-Saxonism?"*

A song came into her head, a silly Yiddish song, and all in all it seemed simplest to sing it out loud, "Oy! Oy! Oy!/Shiker iz a Goy!. . . " while her clothes fled away, all except for her scarf. . . . "Shiker iz er/Trikn miz er/Vayl er iz a Goy!" . . . and then even the scarf abandoned her. And meanwhile a deep voice was moaning, partly in comprehensible English, "My princess," and what could not be understood must have been a kind of English too.

And again. "Oy! Oy! Oy! . . . "

When Dinah woke up, she was alone on a white sheet in a white room. Even the furniture was painted white. She touched her own white skin. . . . Black hair; black, black; black . . . red, red . . .

A hundred dollar bill was on the bedside table.

There was female clothing on the floor. She recognized the 70 denier panty hose in the way you recognize a relative you meet only at funerals.

She groped and the scarf found her fingers. *"At least my scarf understands me."* She wiped herself down with it.

Needing to pee, she went to the connecting bathroom. The hundred dollar bill made excellent toilet paper; she flushed it away.

She felt rather better. The world was hardly spinning at all.

Back in the bedroom, she threw the sticky scarf at the white wall; it clung there, spelling out some cursive symbol in an alphabet that wasn't Hebrew and she didn't think was English either.

Meanwhile a phone was ringing. Just by listening, she found her handbag—it had fallen behind the headboard—and felt a little proud of herself. It didn't occur to her to answer the phone. The ringing ceased.

Elsewhere an artificial voice was going: *"The number you have dialed is unavailable."*

She knew she couldn't stay here, in this interim, forever. Sooner or later she would have to go out into the world. And since she could not hope to disguise what had happened to her body, there was only one thing for it.

She wasn't so gullible as to believe what is written on a cosmetics label—but who or what else could she trust?

She took out the face pack. The Twelve Essential Minerals. She trembled. Her right fist gripped the tube tight and pressed it, until her left palm was rewarded with a blob of dark mud, which she dabbed on this cheek, on that cheek; and she kept squeezing and kept applying the Ahava—on nose, chin, ears, the circumference of the neck, the forehead as high as the hairline, throat down to the collarbone—everywhere on the face indeed apart from the eyeballs, the nostrils, the slit between the lips. The stuff tugged her tiniest hairs and sucked at her pores. And within seconds the outermost layer of the mud had begun to dry, forming a cracked crust, an overskin.

She knew there was a full-length mirror somewhere. There had to be. She had never been in a fancy hotel before, but somehow—call it female intuition—she was convinced of this one fact. She dragged her body around the suite, its three rooms, in search of what she was sure existed—but nowhere, wherever she looked, in bedroom, bathroom, or dressing room, could she see anything like herself.

I May Be a Ghost But I'm Not a Slut

∽ **There were several of us in the "101"**—a bar/café in the Florentin district of Tel Aviv—keeping ourselves to ourselves, just looking on. Now, Florentin is said to be the trendiest neighborhood in the city, and the "101" aspires to be the hottest address within it, so you'd imagine the place would attract a pretty exclusive clientele; but this was August, midafternoon: they have to take what they can get.

The waitresses were wearing black, of course. Lots of leg and cheekbones, they could pass for models. The one leaning against the bar was eyeing the scene dreamily. The other was prowling between the tables. Both of them had blank faces: the burden of their emotions was taken on by their breasts, on show through the translucent material of the blouses. The leaner's nipples tipped up, disdainfully. The prowler's slumped. . . . Then, ten minutes later, the waitresses swapped roles. Now the leaner prowled and the prowler leaned. And their nipples too changed expressions.

At an outside table near the front, not in the shade, a middle-aged man, Amram, rumpled, unshaven, was paying no attention to these subtleties. As far as he was concerned, this café was as good as any other. Now and again he waved half-heartedly at whichever waitress was on prowl-duty: he wasn't in a particular hurry: no doubt somebody'd get around to serving him in the end.

He lit up a Noblesse. He gulped smoke. He knew he wasn't doing himself a favor. He'd been warned against it. Not that doctors really know anything, anyway. Besides, he reckoned he'd reached the age when a man is entitled to feel lousy.

He half-yawned, half-coughed.

"Tired?"

The voice was female. A skinny dark girl was at the next table. She was dressed in solid black—not old-woman black.

"Yes."

"Me too. I'm dead tired."

"Is that so?"

He wondered her age. Schoolgirl? College? Or was she doing her service? It was hard to tell, these days. Sallow complexion: her parents might be from Iraq perhaps, or even from Bukhara; she'd whitened her face with some sort of powdery cosmetic, which didn't go with her skin tone at all. Of course she spoke with the dropped "h" and gargled "r" that all the local kids put on these days, trying to sound worse educated than they actually are.

"Going to bed soon?" she said.

"No. I only just got up."

It occurred to him that maybe she was flirting: but surely not. He had few illusions.

"I'm on night shift," he explained.

"Oh lucky you!"

"You think so?"

"Sure. You get to see life in the dark, when all the wild people come out. Cool!"

"I guess . . ."

"What do you do?"

What did he do? Mossad agent? Professional owl tamer?

"I'm a driver," he confessed. "Ambulance driver."

"Yes, I know."

"How do you know?"

"You're wearing the uniform."

"Now aren't you a smart girl!"

Strange he hadn't realized: he wore it all the time, so he didn't even notice it any more.

"It's a good job," he stressed, as if trying to convince someone.

She watched him, in silence.

"Smoke?" he offered.

She shook her head.

"You're very wise."

Making more show than usual, he snapped his fingers for the waitress.

"Espresso," he said.

"I'll have a Diet Coke," the girl muttered.

"And give the lady what she wants," he said loudly.

After the waitress had wandered away, the girl said:

"It's like . . . "

"It's like," he mimicked her. He hated the way girls nowadays said "like" all the time. "'Like' what?"

"Like nothing," she said, humbled. ". . . How did you get into it, the ambulance driving?"

"Oh, it just happened. In my service I was in the medical corps, drove an ambulance then. And I kept doing it afterwards. When I'm back doing my reserve duty, guess what they make me do? Drive an ambulance, that's right."

The girl said, "You drive many dead people?"

"Sure. Sometimes they're dead when we pick them up. Sometimes they're alive, but they die on us before we get them to the hospital. . . . And what about you? Are you doing your service?"

"Oh, I got myself an exemption. All my friends, we get ourselves exemptions."

"And you're proud of that, are you?"

"No but you see if—"

"So you're a student?"

"No . . . "

"Got a job?"

"No . . . "

"You're just hanging around, are you?"

"No, I . . . "

"What, then?"

She pushed her long hair back. She had fixed it so the hair didn't flow—it seemed to move in one piece, like a block of wood.

"I was thinking of maybe traveling. . . ."

"Where?"

"I was just thinking . . . "

"Big Ben? Taj Mahal? Eiffel Tower? Statue of Liberty? Everest?"

"Whatever. . . . "

Amram snorted. "My generation, we cared, we believed in things—"

"Oh yes?"

"We fought in the Wars."

"You were in battle?"

"Yeah, I was in Lebanon. And I was on the Syrian front in '73, also."

"'73! Hey you're old enough to be my Daddy!"

"Yeah, doesn't it just turn you on?"

She blushed. "I don't think you're being polite."

"Well you don't have to talk to me then."

He looked at this girl—pretty enough, nothing special—and he thought about his job. The worst thing: not the corpses, not as such: loading them on a stretcher, driving them, unloading them at the mortuary. No, it's that after a while you stopped thinking of them as people . . . just a day's work to do, a weight to lift . . . you're grateful when the corpse is skinny . . . your mind drifts to what you're having for supper, and Betar Jerusalem versus Hapoel Tel Aviv—does anybody know the half-time score?

Through his thoughts, the way you hear voices underwater, he heard her say:

"You get many suicides?"

"What?"

"Suicides. You know . . . "

"Yes, lady, I know what a suicide is. . . . Old people, for the most part. There was this couple a few weeks ago, from Bessarabia originally, they were in their eighties: he had Parkinson's, she had congestive heart failure, things were only going to get worse. So he had a pistol, legal, because they had their home across the Green Line, in Bet Shemesh. . . . Her, then himself. You can't blame them."

She shuddered, not altogether unhappily.

"And the mess. . . . People don't realize what a mess they leave for others."

The espresso arrived.

"But the good news is, most of them, the suicides, they fail. It's like . . . last week we had a man, maybe fifty, he'd swallowed barbiturates, then we pumped out his stomach, and he said . . . We brought him back to life, and he said, 'Where's my false teeth?'! Well you've got to laugh."

"Do they do it for love?"

"What?"

"Love? Is that why they do their suicides?"

"No. Who knows? I mean, I'm not a social worker or a rabbi. I bring them in. Somebody else tries to fix them up. . . . How come you're so interested anyway?"

She faced away from him, into the dusty road, the traffic.

"I often think about—"

"I often think about winning the lottery, but it's not going to happen."

"I might do that, the death thing."

"I might be Moshe Dayan," he said, "but I'm not."

"You're laughing at me," she accused him.

"I'm laughing? Look at my face. You call this a laugh?"

"Why do you hate me?"

"I don't hate you. I . . . When I was your age, we dreamed about becoming a sports star or a war hero or a great lover. Now all you've got to dream about is doing yourself in. Get a life!"

"You wouldn't say that if I was dead!"

"Madam. The sun is shining. You are sitting here, drinking a . . . Where is your goddamn drink? Waitress! Waitress! Where is our Diet Coke?" He wiped his brow with the back of his hand.

The waitress brought the Coke over.

Amram rapped his cup against her glass, toasting her, dark drink next to dark drink.

"L'Chaim!"

He took a thoughtful sip.

"Now what were we talking about? . . . Sun . . . Arabs . . . Moshe Dayan . . . Oh yes, you going around killing yourself. A likely story! And you're not telling me you really want to be dead. Dead people have no fun. Dead people don't drink Diet Coke, wear a pushup bra, and have their navel pierced."

Sexily but somehow also shyly, she took his hand and placed it over her navel, figleafing it. Her skin was warm and moved as she breathed.

Hmm, she was cute but not his type. He liked a woman with meat. But still, not bad really . . . And it's not as if he was the kind of man who slept around. He hadn't done that kind of thing for years, not since his army days; and everybody knows that what you do when you're a soldier doesn't count. . . . He could feel his heart inside his rib cage: it was beating uncomfortably fast. Had his body aged faster than his desire? He forced himself to take several slow, long breaths.

She said, "I am dead. As a matter of fact, you're the only person in '101' who can see me."

He laughed. A painful laugh from deep within.

She stared at him, deadpan.

His hand slid away.

She said, "You don't have to believe me."

"No, I believe you. . . . I'll tell you what. If you're invisible, prove it! Take off all your clothes, and dance on the table!"

"I may be a ghost but I'm not a slut!"

Up went his hands, surrendering.

"Okay, I apologize. I guess I got carried away."

His hands wobbled on high . . . He brought them down.

"You're sure you don't want a Noblesse?"

She took out a compact, and adjusted her black lipstick and eyeliner.

"So what did you suicide about?" he asked, playing along. "Love, was it?"

"He's a businessman. He lives in Ramat Aviv Gimel. He told me he'd leave his wife for me, but of course he's a liar."

"Well, these things happen. You'll know better next time."

She pressed a napkin with the name of the café against her lips, wiping off excess lipstick.

Then she took a black envelope from her bag, with an address and a smiley face written on the front in silver marker pen.

"I want you to deliver this."

"What's with you? You think I work for the post office? I move sick and dead people about, not letters."

"It's personal."

"I'm sure it is. You can deliver it yourself."

"It's a suicide note."

"Well there you are then. It'll be more convincing, coming from you."

She pushed it across the table to him.

He toyed with the envelope. She stared at him until he opened it and read it. He shook his head.

"This is terrible, your handwriting. What do they teach you in school? You don't spell suicide like that, you've got completely the wrong consonant. No, seriously, if you want to send it, put it in the post."

"Please . . . Your uniform . . . You can say you found it on the body. It's kind of not really a lie," she said, tucking the letter in her cleavage. "Go on. Take."

Her manner was strangely maternal, he thought, like that of a mother urging her son to eat. Well, if it mattered so much to her . . .

He took the letter, touching her breasts hardly at all. "You're married, aren't you?" she said.

"I'm a—"

"You don't have to say anything. Don't try to lie." She added, "Besides, last time he told me never to do it again."

"You sent him a suicide note before?"

"Only once."

He put the letter back on the table between them.

"Lady, we all have problems. In my case, I'm hot. I want a glass of water. I want to pay and leave. I want the waitress to come. Waitress! Waitress!"

He was half-rising from his chair. No waitress appeared.

He sank back. He mopped his forehead with a handkerchief.

He said, "Listen, this is just some childish fantasy of yours."

"It used to be."

"And both of us, you and me, we've got better things to do than play along with your fantasy."

Distantly, quoting some phrase she'd been taught long ago: "If you will it, it is no dream."

If you will it, it is no dream. Reluctantly, even against his will, he turned his chair so their knees touched. The chair legs scraped on the floor. He didn't look into her eyes. The cosmetic on her cheek was a kind of dust, like on an object in a store-room.

In a new voice, quiet, he said:

"Who are you?"

"Dafna."

"Dafna, that's a pretty name."

"It's the only name I've got."

"My name is Am—. . . uh . . . call me Avraham."

She didn't say anything, neither echoing nor denying.

"Dafna, I know what you want."

She nodded.

"My ambulance, it's parked around the corner. My shift doesn't start till five, not unless I get an emergency call." His voice became slower and higher, wheedling. "Listen, Dafna. I can put you on the stretcher, just like we do with real dead people. And I can strap you down, if you want. And I can put a blanket over you, covering your face."

She nodded again.

"Now. Go ahead of me. I'll meet you one block from here, in front of the Sonol station."

She got up and left. He watched her: the sway of her legs on her platform shoes, her paltry behind.

Alone, he murmured her name (if it was her name), "Dafna." Then, testing the phrase on his lips, "Amram loves Dafna." He smiled at himself. "Dafna Dafna Dafna Dafna..." until the syllables had no meaning at all.

"Waitress!"

For a while neither was available, and then—like buses at a bus stop—one waitress rolled up behind the other.

"I'll pay for my coffee, and I'll pay for whatever the girl in black had."

They looked puzzled.

While he was fumbling for his wallet, a cough began: at first mild, polite—then more intense—he couldn't master it—it was no longer his to stop.

Air found its way back into his lungs.

He levered himself upright.

He spat on the curb.

Slapped down a fifty shekel note—"Keep the change!"—and panting, he shuffled off as fast as he still was able.

The two waitresses cleared and wiped the table between them, and returned to the bar.

"What girl in black?" the upward-pointing nipples said.

"Big tip," said the downward-pointing nipples.

Alte Zakhen

꒳ **The sinners were dancing the rhumba inside a blacked-out** room on the semi-basement level of an unmarked building at the junction of Jaffa Road and King George V, a particular Saturday afternoon in June 1948. The building concealed the Hotel New Jerusalem—exterior signs had been removed in a vain attempt to avoid unwanted attention. The dance was taking place during one of those cease-fires that kept happening that season of that year—temporary, incredible, not to be relied upon—peace flickery and maddening as a malaria dream.

Outside, in most of the rest of West Jerusalem, it was Sabbath. The shops and cafés and restaurants were shut. A Hassid—bearded, in black frock coat and a broad velvet *biber* hat, an old-looking man but not old—was dutifully throwing a stone at the exterior of the ballroom. Music (forbidden on this day) was leaking through. "Shabos! Shabos!" he cried (*Sabbath! Sabbath!*). Of course the window was protected with a bulletproof steel shutter. If his stone had broken through and disturbed the revelry, it would have been a miracle. All the same, he felt impelled to do what he had to do.

As for the sinners: no, they did not repent.

What she remembered, then, was the loud sudden bang on the shutter near her head; not so loud, actually, compared to the music; the music, yes, the jazzy swing of it. And the reddish-greenish spotlights that were doing terrible things to flesh tones—skin reduced to mud—the Hungarian drummer, his lips thick and his nose broad as a Negro's: the Negro fiddler, his heavy-lidded eyes soulful as in any Chagall vision. The passionate or ho-hum swerve of the dancers. The stifling heat: its accompanying perfume of nervous sweat. There was a speakeasy feel to the place. Was it because those present knew their simple pleasure was, in the opinion of others, illicit? Was this what made the afternoon so sweet, so poignant? Or was it rather that on all sides of them, in space and time, danger loomed? Or, when all is said and done, was the intense bittersweet joy a lie: conjured up merely in retrospect?

Yes, these are some of the things she remembered: daylight still outside, but a twilit gloom within. The taxi-dancers. The onlookers. The bang on the shutter: a signal from the exterior world. Also the band—refugees from Mitteleuropa (how had the trumpeter managed to smuggle so much breath out of suffering Europe?), and the lone Negro (what was he doing here, in a conflict that was not his? how had he tumbled in from his own dark continent?).

The rhumba. And then came the foxtrot. Which everybody

who has a mind to can dance to—swaying, sidestepping, turning—some couples do it close together, and others distant. On a red plush banquette in a corner, a group of eight, no seven, Haganah fighters, five men and two women, were huddled earnestly, talking medium-term strategy, she supposed, their Sten guns only partly concealed under linen napkins (a courtesy, merely), the barrels and stocks playing peekaboo. . . .

And meanwhile, outside on King George, a secondhand dealer was swatting his donkey with a stick from an olive tree, a few green leaves still attached, crying, "Alte zakhen!" (*Old things!* in Yiddish). Not that he spoke any Yiddish necessarily, apart from those two words; for, from the first Zionist settlement to the present-day State of Israel, the cry uttered by dealers in old rags, old iron, used goods of any kind . . . a code word shared by Jew and Armenian and Arab, by Ashkenazi and Sephardi, by those who have forgotten and by those who never knew its literal meaning, is always "Alte zakhen!" The donkey was dragging a cart far from full, holding a couple of torn floral curtains, a mattress with its springs rusting through, miscellaneous metallic objects. "Alte zakhen!"

While the dealer was heading up King George, the Hassid (who had triangulated around to Agrippas and back) was on Jaffa Road. They coincided outside the Hotel New Jerusalem.

The Hassid squinted at the dealer. "Bist du a yid?" he asked in Yiddish. (*Are you a Jew?*) And then the same in Hebrew: "Atah yehudi?" Let us suppose for the sake of argument that the dealer understood this question, how should he answer? If yes, that he was a Jew, out plying his trade on the Sabbath, would he not be liable to be stoned? If no, then, taken for an Arab, likewise? The dealer lifted his frayed straw hat momentarily, revealing his oddly unwrinkled face, as if by way of greeting. "Alte zakhen!" he cried out, and continued on his way.

Meanwhile, indoors, a UN representative was ordering scotch on the rocks. A fat man in a fatter suit. There was little scotch in Jerusalem at that moment, and not a great deal of ice; but still, if it could be found anywhere, it would be here, in the busy implausible ballroom of the hotel. . . . A waiter shrugged and went in search of the necessaries.

The night–day. The shivery heat. Like what being inside a balloon might be like, a hot-air balloon—the walls bow and expand slightly and tremble—the very room is afloat, suspended in midmemory. . . .

The past is real, and the future might be real. But the present, always on the point of ceasing to be . . . the only way of coping is not to think about it—focus the mind elsewhen, and she will find she has done whatever it was she had intended.

She remembered this rule, the rule she had instructed herself. And that, a few minutes later, his breath smelling of whiskey, he and she were lindyhopping together. A fat man, yes, but he could move quite delicately and even at times with grace and strength, "lifting" her, "tossing" her between his legs— though of course this was an illusion—without her cooperation, her willingness, her assistance in letting herself be moved about, none of this ingenious motion could have happened.

So this was how she was spending a portion of her afternoon—slipping and twitching about the dance floor with the fat man from the UN—the Hungarian drummer smashing at the cymbals—the Negro fiddler winking at her—the panted small talk between man and woman, ancient as Adam and Eve and the serpent. "Do you come here often?" "You have beautiful skin." "Tell me about your negotiations."

And then the Lambeth Walk. The dance that had been all the rage a decade previously, that had swept across Europe at the time of the Munich Crisis. A novelty dance—a cross between dancing and amateur theatricals, really—the participants pretending to be Cockney fun-lovers. Sheerest nostalgia. The dancers forming parallel lines, men facing women. Much raising of elbow and knee. A skinny young man in a dinner suit singing out the stanzas and the chorus, in English with an accent that sounded more Brooklyn than Lambeth. Finally she and the UN man raising their thumbs at one another and joining in with the communal shout of *Oi!* (Not a Jewish "Oi!" but a Cockney "Oi!"—she had to remember this.)

She remembered this. She was aware of this. Things she observed personally and things she could never have observed personally. The drummer raising a single drumstick high in the air; the trumpet held up to the light. The Hassid and the dealer, each tramping and jolting along in predestined paths around all but deserted streets, in their separate, considered motions, beyond the ballroom walls. The fat man's uncircumcised penis staring out at her, inside a stall in the gentlemen's lavatory. His trousers and underpants were loose around his ankles. The English sentence she had memorized: *If you do not do everything I will tell you, I will shoot you in the balls.* Was it her own voice that she heard: accented, awkward, strained with the effort of trying not to (queer that she felt the urge to laugh) laugh? Laugh! It was as much as she could do to keep the revolver level, while simultaneously getting her tongue around those consonant-packed English syllables. Did she succeed? She thought perhaps she had said *suit you in the balls*. Not that there was anything she could do about it. Repeating the sentence would have been more than flesh and blood could bear. No prompter, here and now. No possibility of taking a short break, gulping a glass of water, and going back to the top of the page. No, small mistakes don't count. She was doing what she had to, near enough. Talking into his penis as if into a microphone. *He's* the one who should be nervous. Why wasn't *he* laughing? Did he really not get the joke?

She tied his wrists behind him, with his own striped necktie. She gagged him with a linen napkin monogrammed Hotel New Jerusalem. Oddly, his erection had not wilted; it projected as far as, farther than his paunch; this was something she had not envisaged would happen, it had never been mentioned in the briefings and the training sessions, the preenactments. How awkward to lift and heave his underpants and trousers, to do up the column of buttons, to fasten the belt. The cavalry twill cloth stuck out, like a tent, even as she murmured her second line, *I could kill you at any moment*.

She remembered this. And she remembered being out on the quiet streets, as dusk was beginning to fall (the air had not yet cooled, but it was less humid here than inside). Her ears were still ringing from the noise of the band, as if from gunfire (of course her gun had *not* been fired, that would have ruined everything, but she nevertheless felt the as it were effects of a recoil: a buzzing flutter in her wrist, a phantom ache in her armpit). The representative of the United Nations was walking an inch in front of her, sweating, obedient, the barrel of her revolver was pressed against the small of his back. And then the Hassid took out his M-1, covering her, and the secondhand dealer helped her roll the UN man into the back of his donkey cart. Next, she and the Hassid climbed in too: they lay down on either side of the UN man—like mother and father with the baby between them. She did her best to tug the ruined curtain over the three of them (the Hassid making no effort to help her; was this considered a woman's task?).

Her and her accomplice's guns were pressed against the head and belly of the man in the middle, who had squeezed his eyes shut, whether out of fear or ostrichlike, to make his fate go away—yet somehow he could not, or would not, rid himself of his erection. His one instinctive act of defiance. *I am not altogether in agreement with your point of view* is how he would have diplomatically phrased what the body stated so crudely. She did consider answering him, adding a note of not quite apology but at least explanation: *I'm not myself, right now . . .* but she doubted her English was up to it; and in any case she wasn't at all sure it would be proper for her to address him: she had never told him her real name, so strictly speaking they had not been introduced. She heard the thwack as the dealer brought his olive switch down on the donkey's flank; next he made a clicking noise with tongue against the roof of his mouth, to drive the beast on. An international sound, in human–donkey pidgin. She heard all this—the click equally loud as the thwack, to her ears, in her memory. She felt the cart stir and tilt, the clatter of horseshoes on paving . . . as four humans and an animal shifted off down Jaffa Road.

And meanwhile, within the ballroom of the grandest hotel still functioning in West Jerusalem, Sabbath had come to an end. The balloon had come to earth, its fabric sagging. The former dancers were enjoined to enact a version of the Havadalah ritual, customary at this hour. The jazz band was striking up the traditional melodies: Shavua Tov *(Good Week)* and then Eliyahu HaNavi *(Elijah the Prophet . . . may he come to us, with the Messiah, the descendant of David . . .)*, while, in accordance with tradition, the celebrants were passing around a silver container pierced with tiny holes, in the shape of the Tower of David, flying a brave stiff flag; this each man and woman sniffed in turn, eyes narrowed, inhaling the sweetness of cloves and nutmeg and cinnamon.

Finally a dozen or twenty candles appeared: elaborate plaited candles of red and white wax: these were held up by the sinners (who, since Sabbath was now over, technically no longer qualified as sinners, perhaps). The electric lights were turned off. The candles were alight. All that could be seen was the glow of the flames and what they illuminated: a flickery gleam on musical instruments of metal and of wood, and on the wooden floor, and on hands and wrists and faces—this too is what she remembered, what she would never forget until her dying day, for all that, while the ceremony took place, she was no longer there.

The Moving Business

❧ **He was never seen again. In the predawn semigloom,** silhouetted against a razor-wire fence, at the agreed coordinates in the Bekaa Valley—while mud spattered from a misdirected rocket-propelled grenade, and a mortar made planet Earth shudder in its orbit—somebody claimed to have glimpsed him. About five minutes later the entire infiltrating force was evacuated from the vicinity of the supposed Hizbullah base by helicopter gunship—including two corpses and three wounded, one critically—but excluding him. It had been a botched operation, right from the start.

His name had been Ehud. He had been a private in the Israeli Army.

He qualified for no funeral; a service of commemoration instead. His commanding officer delivered the eulogy. How

Ehud had been a martyr. How Ehud is the model the rest of us can aspire to. How Ehud exemplified all that is noblest in the Zionist ideal. How "...Let us recall the last words of Trumpeldor, treacherously slain at Tel Hai: *It is good to die for our country!...*" Amen. Silence.

Though when all's said and done, there had been nothing so outstanding about the man. A conscript, doing what he had to. And, back when he was alive, some had wondered why he had ever been accepted into the elite paratroops. Sure, he was rugged enough. And it helped that he spoke fluent Arabic (his father had been born in Aleppo). But he smoked too much hash, and he was always among the last to volunteer for any duties. Still, it's not as if there is a national surplus of heroes— we must take them where we can find them.

Nobody knew this better than his ... girlfriend would be too strong a term. She was an operational assistant attached to the unit. A sergeant in intelligence. A secretary, in practice. She was kept busy filing reports, doing basic bookkeeping, making sure each soldier received his top secret instructions on time and that they were destroyed afterwards—half her waking hours were spent scurrying between the photocopier and the shredding machine. She and Ehud had made love ... how many times? Fewer than the fingers on two hands. Quite possibly, probably, in the throes of passion, she or he had murmured "I love you!" That was about as far as it went.

His eighteenth birthday had taken place a couple of weeks earlier. She had given him a printout—something she had downloaded from the Internet—showing a soldier with an

M–16 thrusting from his crotch, and the legend *Paratroops Do It With Their Weapons!* It had seemed not very funny even then—but as a woman surrounded by men, she had felt the need to give as good as she got.

What else can be said about their relationship? He was good-looking, amiable, with a dazzling smile, needed taking care of. She was short and dark; as a teenager she'd had a gamine charm—but in the army she'd put on weight, as women do—she was not generally considered much of a catch.

Anyway, after the memorial service—her muscles aching from standing at attention so long—she returned to base with all the others. She spooned twice the usual dose into the *finjan* and cooked up strong Turkish coffee.

Nobody said much. The men drank down their coffee and ate their Krembo treats. A few looked up at her and smiled sympathetically, but not as sympathetically as all that. Everybody knew she didn't qualify as an honorary widow. Besides, she'd merely lost a lover: they had lost a comrade in arms. . . . No doubt some of them couldn't help wondering who'd get to fuck her next.

A year later her service was over. She had no particular plans or ambitions. Her future was unclear, like when you dream you are waking from a dream. She guessed that—like many ex-soldiers—she might as well travel.

And while she was at it . . . there was something she'd kept to herself. Ehud had confided in her, the night before he'd disappeared, that he was thinking of deserting. He'd had it up to here. He wanted out. Of course he was high on hash and speed and ecstasy at the time—his talk shouldn't be taken that seriously—and quite possibly five hours later, as he was parachuting into Lebanon, he'd completely forgotten he'd ever so much as toyed with the notion—and it wasn't as if she knew anything for certain—and it's absolutely not the kind of thing you can accuse a fallen hero of. . . . All the same, she reckoned she might as well make some attempt to find Ehud.

She tried to think herself into his mind. If he were deserting, where would he go? He had connections with Lebanese drug traffickers—so probably he'd take the heroin route in reverse, heading up across the Turkish border, via Iskenderun and Antâkya, making for Istanbul. . . .

She flew to Istanbul. She stayed at a cheap hotel in the old town. She visited the Blue Mosque and the Topkapi Palace. She persuaded a stranger to take a photograph of her standing in front of an ancient doorway. She enjoyed a real Turkish bath. She ate a falafel at the Netanya Café on Divan Yolu, near the intersection with Hippodrome Street, where all the Israeli backpackers hang out. She asked around, without giving too much away herself. . . . No definite information, but yes, several travelers had run into somebody who looked more or less like Ehud, some of whom were even called Ehud (it's a common enough Israeli name)—she had a number of leads to follow. . . .

She overlanded by train and bus to Antalya, and sought out the Israeli package tourists soaking up rays on the beach. After about a week her skin had darkened a shade, and passersby addressed her in Turkish. She speculated he might have found himself a job here. Again: some hints, but no solid clue.

So she flew on to Delhi . . . Agra . . . down through Rajasthan to Goa (weeks or months went by idyllically on the beach at

Palolem, of which she later remembered almost nothing, apart from eating prawn vindaloo, drinking *feni*, and smoking hash; and the locals crossing themselves as they made *puja* to the dawn sun) . . . back via Varanasi . . . Dharamsala . . . Sikkim (which was heaven) . . . doing what travelers in India are supposed to do, but all the while asking about Ehud. India, she thought, is where he very well might have ended up, like tens of thousands of other aimless Israelis. When you are in India, it is hard to believe there was a time when you were not in India: hard to conceive of a time when you will no longer be in India.

But her journey was far from over. From Sikkim she roughed it to Nepal; and thence flew by way of Dhaka to Bangkok . . . headed down to Ko Pha Ngan for the New Moon Rave—exactly the kind of event where Ehud would be, but he wasn't—and ended up staying at Paradise Bungalows for several weeks; until she bought ecstasy from an informer: and the police made her pay the usual fifty thousand baht bribe. . . . So she headed back up through Laos; down the Mekong to Luang Prabang . . . and somehow she found herself in Angkor Wat. The ancient monuments astounded her. Her mind was filled with fantastic visions and longing. . . .

And she arrived in Hong Kong with her savings exhausted. She got hired as an illegal barmaid at the Cat and Fiddle in Kowloon. She found a shared apartment among the semihippies on Lamma Island. She stayed for six months. It wasn't too bad. She could nearly imagine living here. It's true that some of the customers were rude; more than once a businessman assumed she moonlighted as a prostitute, and when she turned him down, he'd go, "Who wants to fuck you, you fat tart?" But others were okay—she had one-night stands with a Hungarian toy importer and a New Zealander in the drain-cleaning line, also with a Chinese man who said his name was Ling, because after all she was in the Far East and it would be a shame not to have had done it at least once. And she had a kind of on–off relationship with Shane, a construction worker from Liverpool who lived near her on Lamma. And now and again she'd run into an Israeli passing through; she enjoyed talking Hebrew, and swapping gossip, and she'd always inquire if he or she happened to have run into somebody who fitted Ehud's description. But Hong Kong can be confining, if you have no good reason to be there; a well-decorated prison. She figured she had traveled long enough—she might as well go home. . . . But how could she? She had not yet found Ehud.

On to Tokyo. Where she hooked up with a bunch of Israelis involved in the phony designer gear racket in collaboration with the *yakuza*. Of course these weren't the kind who'd served in elite units—they'd bribed and faked their way out of the IDF, or had done time as grease-monkeys and military dishwashers. All the same, in their faux-toughness, their disdain for any authority other than that of the group, their comradeliness, they reminded her of her days in the paratroops. She stayed a couple of months with them, in their tiny apartment in Ebisu, helping out by sewing mock Levi-Strauss labels onto jeans. . . . None of them had ever heard of Ehud.

Next, Los Angeles. The sun and beach life reminded her of Tel Aviv. And it was impossible to park your car anywhere without hearing somebody chattering away in Hebrew, or so it seemed to her. She hadn't come across such a high concentration of Israelis since Dharamsala. She lived in a hostel on Venice Beach. She made a living doing hair-wraps on the boardwalk. Of course she asked casually about Ehud. . . . Yes, there were suggestions that somebody who looked like him might be somewhere in the Los Angeles area . . . intelligence of a sort, unclear as ever.

Actually Los Angeles appealed to her. Something like Israel only not Israel. Life Lite. In Hebrew the world is divided into "Within the Land" and "Outside the Land"—no need to say which land is meant. If you are going to be "Outside the Land" then one place is as good as another—so why not L.A.?

The routine was addictive. She had a romance with a wannabe star, who was currently playing a minor role in a soap opera. A Viking type, blond and blue-eyed. (When she told him she'd been in Israeli Intelligence, a kingpin in secret operations, this turned him on. She didn't exactly lie, but she let him get the impression she'd been in the thick of every mission. He was a body builder, massively muscled, tall. He liked her to "capture" him, yell at him in Hebrew, and tie him down.) She could readily have stayed here . . . but there was so much more of the world to see—and she had not yet found Ehud.

She waited until winter was over. And then, in March 2002, she flew into New York. She contacted Israelis in Manhattan— friends from home; and friends she'd met along her way; and friends of friends; and friends of friends of friends. . . . For a few months she hung out in the East Village scene. . . . She moved to a loft on the Greenpoint/Williamsburg border, and mingled with the artist types. . . . She checked out the Sephardim along King's Highway. . . .

And finally, one afternoon in May, she was standing by a not very busy intersection in Forest Hills, Queens. A van from the Masada moving company was parked there. Some men in jeans and T-shirts were schlepping a bed and a cocktail cabinet and a chest-of-drawers and a stuffed giraffe out of a suburban home. She waited under a leafless plane tree in the strong noon light. The men were stumbling, and swearing in Hebrew.

At last they took a break. One man went and sat by the fence, on top of a crated Sony television. He lit up a Marlboro.

"Shalom, Ehud."

"Shalom." He didn't seem surprised to see her. He said in Hebrew, "Hey, Naomi, how's it going?"

She sat beside him on the crate. He offered her a cigarette, but she told him she had given up smoking—her last puff had been en route from Sikkim to Nepal. He offered her a joint, but she turned that down too.

Then it was her turn to ask a few questions. He told her what had happened, briefly. It wasn't that remarkable. He'd run away from the battle; hidden out till daybreak. Then, well—he had a Canadian passport; hadn't he mentioned it? his mother was from Montreal—he'd hitched to Beirut, caught a plane via Cyprus and Athens to New York. And that's where he'd been ever since, living in Queens and Long Island, working as an illegal, doing moving jobs . . . and frankly he'd had enough of it: yeah, he wanted to go back home, to Israel, to settle down with a good woman.

She gave him a steady look—this man, rumpled, paunchy, sweaty, red-eyed, his hair thinning . . . Then she closed her eyes, and envisioned Ehud: the hero: young and strong, handsome and brave.

Naomi opened her eyes. She stood up.

She said to him in English, "I'm sorry. There's been a mistake. I thought you were someone I knew. . . ."

She caught a cab to JFK; and from there she flew on to Panama City, and trekked south into the Central American jungle. There were some leads suggesting the true Ehud might be found there, perhaps.

Hatikvah

⌒: **Have you ever been nowhere in particular? An airport,**
let's say? In the year that might have been 2000? Did you see
and hear (just for a minute) a couple of strangers, typical as
any? You were hurrying through Departures. You paid little
attention to them, and almost certainly you and they will never
coincide again.... Tell everything that you know about them,
and everything that you don't know.

⌒:

Their names are Tami and Jaime (known as "Jota"). They
passed through childhood and adolescence in the late 1980s and
1990s in Cape Town and Buenos Aires, respectively. Both are
Jewish. That's about all they have in common. Tami's parents
are middle middle class, and when she was growing up they

owned a not very grand house in the more or less *haimishe* Sea Point district. Her father, like his father before him, made a living buying used clothing from whites and selling it to blacks. The business was doing none too well. The family couldn't afford a live-in maid (not that they wanted one, exactly): there was just a cleaner, Sheila (who looked white but was in fact Cape Colored—"Cape Muslim" you were supposed to start calling them, now), who showed up once a week. You couldn't honestly say Tami's father's family had ever been particularly successful at anything; they'd immigrated from Lithuania a century earlier, drifting south by way of Johannesburg to what had then been the mixed-race District 6. Apartheid had come as a terrible nuisance. "What a gevalt!" her father would keep chuckling, as he narrated a sequence of tragedies and cock-ups.

Her mother's family, however, had had a more romantic past (so Tami reckoned): fleeing a pogrom, they'd ended up in semidesert, the Karoo, farming ostriches of all things—the plumes were invaluable for ladies' hats. They were the kind of Jews known as *Boerejoode*—muddling along in Afrikaans—and her ancestors on that side had been conscripted to fight on the Boer side in the Anglo-Boer war. Her father's family, on the other hand, had been recruited by the British Empire. The vision of her great-grandfathers, in different uniforms, speaking different Yiddish pidgins, waging war against one another, shocked and excited Tami. But that was all way in the past. Everything important had happened long ago. Throughout Tami's life (as best as she could remember) apartheid had been either dying or dead; she had never known it in the days when it had seemed plausibly eternal—a great steel gate you could lean on or kick against—of course she was grateful but, then, she felt she had missed out on something.

This image of ancestors at war would have intrigued Jota's parents, psychoanalysts both. The family lived in a rather remarkable villa in the Palermo Chico district, directly opposite the spacious grounds of the Sociedad Rural, where the upper class trotted by on horseback. Financially successful, certainly, for they were at the peak of their profession; indeed, given the political situation, what could a Porteño do, prudently, better than lie down on the analyst's couch? Of course Jota had only been a baby at the time of the Malvinas campaign, and the downfall of Galtieri. Dictatorship was ancient history. He had never personally suffered as a consequence, nor had any close relative (a second cousin on his father's side, an art student, had been "disappeared"; for that matter the *desaparecidos* had included elder brothers and sisters, uncles and aunts, of a number of his school friends). He had been born too late. . . . Recurrently Jota had dark dreams, and his parents had offered to analyze them—he had always turned down the offer.

Whatever else being Jewish may stand for, it permits an identity additional to being simply Argentinian, simply South African. Not that either Jota's or Tami's family were especially keen on religion. Jota's parents were nominally atheists (they attended the Templo Israelito just on social occasions: marriage and funeral, bar mitzvah and bris). Now and again on a Friday evening Tami had been taken along to the shul; the men had clapped what they called "yarmies" on their heads: the women had paraded their hats (Tami's mother possessed her grandmother's, plumed with ostrich feathers; worn only on High

Holy Days); the praying was over quickly: then they had all had a good schmooze. At any rate, for whatever reason (if only to get the children out of the house on the weekend, somewhere they wouldn't get mugged or take drugs, while the parents did whatever it is parents do) Tami and Jota were sent along to Zionist youth groups.

Tami's was Habonim (literally: "The Builders"). She enjoyed it; most of her friends belonged. They went in for a lot of Israeli folk dancing; somebody would have a go on the guitar and they'd sing pretty songs in Hebrew about farm animals and Jerusalem, peace and love. (They did not speak more than the most minimal Hebrew: they memorized the lyrics phonetically.) There was flirtation, and crushes of various kinds; teenagers would loaf around, staring, their lips protruding and wobbling slightly, in the way South Africans do when trying to appear cute, but nothing much more happened, not least because everybody was always milling about with everybody else. Habonim was vaguely left wing—but not in any way that could cause upset (Tami's mother's brother Joe, a communist, had been forced into exile in London; nobody wanted Tami ending up like that): really it amounted to little more than a fondness for the Kibbutz Ideal and a page having being torn out from the Habonim songbook, which had contained the *Internationale* in Hebrew translation.

While Tami was dancing the hora at Habonim, Jota, in uniform, was standing at attention at Betar. Betar embodied a particular take on Zionism. It's founder, Ze'ev Jabotinsky, had called on European Jews to fight actively against Nazism, and later, in Palestine, against the British. The myth of its origin was important to Betar: "*Ja-bo-tin-sky! Olé! Olé!*" Jota and his comrades chanted. The pugnacious Betar hymn, "Two Banks of the Jordan," advocating territorial expansion, was not sung as often as all that—if only because the lyrics were hard to remember. Betar's detractors accused it of being quasi-Fascist; of supporting anti-Arab terrorism. At any rate, as far as its Buenos Aires branch was concerned, it was not so different from the Scouts, say. There was camping and trekking. There was flirtation and folk dancing in the clubhouse (the *maoz* as it was called; literally, the "fortress"). There were collective trips to the La Boca quarter, to the national soccer stadium known as the Bombonera, where never mind what teams were playing, the Betarniks in unison, disconcerting the other spectators, would yell the cry of Betar's champion sports team in Israel, *"Ba-esh u-va-mayim! Betar Yerushalayim!"* ("Through fire and water! Betar Jerusalem!").

Somewhere in the ideology of these Zionist youth groups was the notion that all Jews should, and maybe would, emigrate to Israel. Maybe, in the millennium that was about to begin, "Jew" would no longer signify a minority, on the move, every so many generations, from place to place—but rather the inhabitants of a particular nation-state. *"Next year in Jeru-salem!"* they intoned collectively in Hebrew, *"Next year in Jerusalem rebuilt!"* This was projected as a wish; in practice, it wasn't to be expected.

For Jota, the idea of living anywhere other than Buenos Aires seemed bizarre: the inhabitants of the rest of the world were surely, to some degree, kidding. His family had always been Porteños (apart from distant cousins who had spent time in a Jewish colony on the pampas, at Moises Ville); presumably they had originally come from Eastern Europe, from the Pale of

Settlement, but the family tree couldn't be traced back nearly so far. All the same, who can see into the future? It was not impossible that Jota might one day choose or have to leave, even as far away as that.

As for Tami, the prospect of going on *aliya* to Israel was definitely in the cards. Many of her childhood friends, her parents' friends, many of the other teenagers at Habonim, had already fled the country—to Perth or Melbourne, London or New York . . . and some indeed to Israel: her best friend from kindergarten had sent her a snapshot showing her new home in Ra'anana, north of Tel Aviv. (So many Jews, in fact, had left Cape Town that the shul her family used to attend had shut down; now they had to drop by a different one on Friday nights, if they chose to go at all.) Not that she really wanted to leave; she cared about her homeland: she loved it.

All the same, it wasn't clear there would be any place for people like her in the new South Africa. What could she contribute anyway? Among her generation, it was the fashion to dismiss political involvement as old-fashioned and pointless— "cough-sweeting" was their term for it (after an advertising poster for Hale's Cough Sweets, showing a white boy giving a black man a sweet). Still, both Jota and Tami lived in places where patriotism was allowed to be positive. At Betar and at Habonim, toward the end of their meetings, the youths would line up and launch into the national anthems of their countries. "¡Oid, Mortales, el grito sagrado/Libertad! Libertad! Libertad! . . . " ("Hear, Mortals, the sacred cry, Liberty! Liberty! Liberty! . . . ")—Jota put his hand over his heart and boomed this in his finest baritone. Meanwhile (though their songbook still contained the former anthem: "The Call Of South Africa/Die Stem

Van Zuid Afrika") Tami and her friends would stammer out the new composite one, with its alternate stanzas in Xhosa and Afrikaans, with feeling. And then there would be a brief pause, for coughing and taking a deep breath, and for thought—followed by their common song, the Israeli national anthem, HaTikvah ("The Hope"). So sing out, then, Tami, Jota, Habonim, Betar, in Cape Town, in Buenos Aires—all together now!—"*Kol od balevav penimah/Nefesh yehudi homiyah...*" ("All the while in the heart/A Jewish soul yearns..."). Take it from there.

Tami and Jota finished high school, and both opted to take a year off before going to university. After thinking it over, both made the decision to spend some time in Israel. For Tami, what would be safest and most obvious would be to go to a kibbutz— but instead of heading along with many fellow South Africans to the one in the Galilee suggested by Habonim, she arranged instead to go to a different one in the Negev, recommended by her old friend in Ra'anana—because she had always wanted to live in the desert. As for Jota, Betar would have preferred him to join the Israeli army—and he would have quite liked that, except that that would be a three-year commitment—so instead he made enquiries about kibbutzim—and he was assigned to one.

So this is how the two of them came together at a kibbutz that shall remain nameless, not too far south of Beersheba.

The kibbutz was a fairly wealthy, fairly well established, fairly large one. There were over four hundred members, including at any given time about eighty volunteers from various countries. The volunteers worked on the date palms, and the aloe vera plantation, and in the plastic bowl factory. They lived in pairs, in prefabricated huts. Saturday was the only nonworking day; so Friday night was for getting drunk; Saturday was for nursing a hangover and, now and then, being taken on trips to see the wonders of the desert—geography and history lessons come to life.

The kibbutzniks pretty much kept to themselves; the volunteers socialized almost exclusively with other volunteers, according to their language groups—so the Anglophones (the majority) hung out together; and the Francophones and the Hispanophones had their own little cliques. Naturally, then, Tami and Jota, though they saw each other often enough, though at times they even worked nearby, bagging the dates or tying back the oozing aloe vera under a burning sun, did not converse; she spoke no Spanish and he almost no English.

But after about a month, Tami and Jota volunteered to join the Ulpan—the language course. This meant they would get to work shorter hours in return for studying Hebrew and committing themselves to stay at the kibbutz for a full six months. In their very first lesson, their teacher (who adopted the sensible approach of pairing up students who had no shared language) ordered the two of them to sit side by side and to become study partners. They were taught how to greet one another in Hebrew. Both together now! Repeat after me! . . . *"Shalom! . . . Shalom, Tami! . . . Shalom, Jota! . . . Shalom shalom!"*

Soon they acquired the ability to say I and You, Yes and No . . . they learned nouns and pronouns . . . past, present, future . . . the many complex forms deriving from a three-consonant verb-stem. . . . By the end of six months, they had reached a fair degree of fluency in spoken Hebrew, and some knowledge of the written language too. . . . When, on Independence Day, the whole kibbutz stood up and sang HaTikvah, Tami and Jota knew not only the words, they knew the meaning of every word.

Ah! *HaTikvah.* Its melody derives from a Bohemian folk tune; its lyrics were composed by an immigrant who stayed in the land for just a few years before heading on to, of all places, India, and converting to, of all faiths, Christianity. It is as kitschy as the national anthem of any other country; nevertheless it is as potent and moving as you want it to be. . . .

Needless to say, they had an affair. (It would have been strange if they had not. Just about every other volunteer was involved in some kind of romance.) To be sure, Tami and Jota did not have a huge amount in common—apart from being Jewish, roughly the same age, volunteers at the same kibbutz, and a long way from home in a place where nobody knew them. They were not especially each other's types: Tami dreamed of a gentle, long-haired boy who would strum a guitar while making the world a better place; Jota's private preference was for blue-eyed blondes (Tami looked too much like his mother). Still, they were content enough together. They said "I love you" in Hebrew, in the male-subject female-object and female-subject male-object versions of that sentence. . . . And in fact, the longer they spent together, the more they discovered they had in common after all. To start with, they were both from the Southern Hemisphere. This may sound trivial—certainly neither would have dreamed of defining him or herself as an Antipodean—but it is not nothing. Without saying a word, each knew the other was disconcerted that August should

be the hottest month here, as they sweated in the early morning raking the ground beneath the date palms. As they strolled
hand in hand at night, beyond the aloe vera fields, they gazed
up at the desert sky rich with constellations neither of them
recognized; then they kissed passionately. . . . Really, if you're
falling into love, anything will do to prove it.

And romance changed everything: henceforward let even
the most familiar sight—the clusters of growing dates band-
aged with taped-on polyethylene sacks—the aloe vera fronds,
stiffly floppy and sticky like the limbs of a feverish child—the
plastic watering cans tumbling from the plastic-watering-can
machine—be strange and wonderful: let their hidden meaning
be revealed to Tami and Jota, only to them.

They found a secret place—a shed lined with fertilizer
sacks—where they would make love. They would begin by
whispering affection in Hebrew, and then in the throes of passion they would babble and scream in their native tongues—no
matter—there was nothing the other did not understand.

After leaving the kibbutz they spent a month together traveling around Israel—from Eilat's crowded beaches to within sight
of the Lebanese border—from the trance clubs of Tel Aviv to
the Judean desert—and then they both wondered what to do
next. In truth Israel had been the backdrop for their experience,
rather than the ground of it: but it didn't always have to be so;
they seriously thought about staying in Israel, about becoming
Israelis; at the least they could apply to the program at the
Hebrew University. . . . But, actually, it would be a lot more
practical to study back home. They could always immigrate

here later.... One day the two of them would meet up again, hopefully.

Tami studied social work at the University of Witwatersrand. She had several minor affairs; then, after her abortion and her lesbian phase, she shacked up with Piet, a high school teacher from Lesotho, and the two of them shared an apartment for a while in Port Elizabeth, until he left her for a sixteen-year-old pupil of his, and she moved to London and lived in a squat in Hackney, and she hitched to the Glastonbury Festival where she met up with a caravan of New Age travelers with whom she set out across Europe, and she joined a touring company performing Shakespeare in Andalusia, before settling down in Barcelona where she got a job teaching English to civil engineers. Jota studied piano and composition at the conservatoire for a year: he transferred to the university where he obtained his degree in accounting. He was recruited by a small but enthusiastic business management concern, specializing in the venture capital field, and, after two years in Buenos Aires, was sent to Santiago de Chile, where he rapidly married and divorced, and at his own request he was once again relocated, this time to New York.

Meanwhile the two of them kept in touch. To begin with they phoned (but this was horrendously expensive) and they sent frequent e-mails and postcards . . . but they were both forgetting their written Hebrew fast . . . so they exchanged cassette tapes . . . but soon even that was beyond them; not to mention that their experiences were so different: how could they ever explain themselves? . . . Communication fell off to a once-a-year card on the anniversary of their first time—and then (when she had departed for Britain and he for Chile) not even that. The lovers had lost touch.

Now it came to pass that Tami's mother (who was still living in the old house in Sea Point) became ill; she had heart problems; she was not expected to survive much longer. So Tami bought a roundtrip ticket to Cape Town. Her job could spare her for just one week. The cheapest flight was on TAP via Lisbon.... And Jota's company was sending him briefly over to Mozambique for an informational visit, to explore investment opportunities there; the only decent connection was via Lisbon.... So the two of them happened to be in the same terminal of the same airport at the same time. They had both shown their passports and gone through to the departure zone. A queerly stressed PA voice was making announcements in three languages. Tami's and Jota's flights were both due to leave in twenty minutes: last boarding had been proclaimed. Somewhere between the newsstand and the duty free shop, each carrying a fairly heavy carry-on bag, Tami and Jota brushed up against one another.

"Excuse me," Jota said in English.

And Tami said the equivalent in Spanish, *"Perdón."*

Then the two of them talked simultaneously: Jota (in English) and Tami (in Spanish) said, "Haven't I seen you before somewhere?" Then Jota (in Spanish) and Tami (in English) repeated much the same question by way of answer.

They really couldn't work out where it might have been. No, Jota had never been in Barcelona nor Tami in New York.... Even exchanging names didn't help, since Jota had since reverted to being known as Jaime, and Tami had actually gone through quite a variety of nicknames in the course of her life.

Then—at the same instant—for no particular reason—each identified the other. The simultaneity and certainty of this revelation gave them a curt intense pleasure—quasi-sexual, one might say; except that neither found the other attractive at all. Tami saw a paunchy, balding businessman; Jota a bedraggled, aging hippie. They spoke of this and that (their lives; the weather; do-you-remember's) in fluent English and in fluent Spanish, and it made no difference, whatever they said, however well they understood what the other was getting at, they lit not one spark of their old romance.

This could not be kept up much longer. Another announcement had come over the system. They really had to make haste, both of them.

Finally, in desperation they tried to communicate in Hebrew. But what could they remember on the spur of the moment? *Shalom*, they could say—they said it several times.... They could barely remember how to say "I love you."... But at least they felt something again—if not love then a sense of the absence where affection had been. How desperately they wanted to communicate—and the two languages they now had in common were worse than useless. They had to gab away in Hebrew—yet how could they?

At last they realized there was only one thing for it. Jota set down his briefcase between his feet. Tami deposited her stripy Thai shoulderbag on the reflective, slick linoleum. Side by side, in the departure zone of a generically anonymous air terminal somewhere in the Diaspora, the pair of ex-lovers sang the only song that was theirs.

"All the while in the heart, a Jewish soul yearns . . ." they sang in Hebrew, at the top of their voices, her soprano and his baritone echoing from floor and ceiling and the Plexiglas partition that marked off the duty free. ". . . Oh, our hope is not lost, / The hope of two thousand years / To live a free people in our land, / The land of Zion and of Jerusalem . . . *Od lo avdah tikvateynu / HaTikvah bat sh'not alpayim / Lihyot am khofshi be'artzeynu / Eretz Tzion v'Yerushalayim!*"

Then—without saying another word—the heartbroken strangers turned their backs on one another. They picked up their belongings and hurried off to catch their next flight.

Mr. Fig and Mr. Pineapple

꙳ **Sometimes in the small hours when I can't sleep, I put the** pillow over my head and I remember my wars. My wife, on the other hand, is a faithful devotee of the television news. She watches it; she absorbs the day's quota of tragedy and hope, and passes it through her system. Then, at midnight, she falls into a deep sleep. On the rare occasions when I have tried to keep her awake past this hour she has resisted. "No, don't stop me! I am Cinderella!"

For my part, however, I am unable to believe in television. When I was a child there was no such thing as television in Israel. (Try telling my children that!) I can't stand the flickering, mumbling box. I sometimes wonder if my problem is that I have a secret fear that television is two-way, watching me at the same time I am watching it.

Be that as it may, I make do with radio. Often I lie in bed beside my shallow-breathing wife, my headphones plugged in, roaming through the channels. Tonight, for instance, I tuned in to Channel 2—but it was playing Mizrachi music, not my thing at all; and then I tried the IDF station—a girlfriend of a soldier in the Givati Brigade was organizing a live on-air birthday party for him, his comrades and friends and relatives were phoning in, notwithstanding that the birthday boy had in fact passed away last week on active service. Channel 1 was no better. And Jordanian Radio was broadcasting the news in French, of all things.

And then I found myself catching a station unknown to me, somewhere out there in the FM band. The speaker had a Yiddish intonation and his Hebrew was archaic; he kept talking about the "Incident." I came to realize this was a broadcast of the Lubavitch Hassidim. Their leader, the Rebbe, suspected of being the Messiah, died some years ago; the Lubavitchers never refer to his "death"—no, nothing so absolute. "Please listen again, same time, same channel, next week, in the event that the exile has not ended and the Messiah has not come." And if I were to tune in next week, and hear nothing, what would I deduce? That the Messiah had arrived? Or would I suppose that the Ministry of Communications had cracked down at long last? This is after all what they call a "pirate" station. . . . Then, finally—a wooden-legged Hassid with a parrot on his shoulder was sailing through my half-consciousness—I drifted off. . . .

The "Incident"—how difficult it is to say more than that. We have a language for evoking and invoking catastrophe. I could tell you about my wars, the three of them I fought for my country. My wife was in two. There has been more war since, and if there is more to come I assure you I will have no problem discussing it. I can, if pressed, scream with the best of them. But how to so much as mention the lesser things . . . that Wednesday three weeks ago, when Amalia and I were walking down Kesarya Street. . . .

Ah, there is so much that must be explained first . . . Amalia . . . Kesarya Street. . . .

You know, don't you, the two fruit shops? Just before where Kesarya unites with Jabotinsky? Why there should be a pair of virtually identical fruit shops side by side I cannot explain; wouldn't it be more sensible to locate them at opposite ends of Jerusalem? But that is how it often is. One must not seek for logic in retail establishments. The names of the fruiterers are . . . but nobody uses their real names. They are universally referred to as Mr. Fig and Mr. Pineapple.

Now Mr. Fig sells low-priced fruit, and vegetables too; the quality is not up to much. (I shop there when I am feeling pinched.) By contrast, Mr. Pineapple is expensive, but sometimes he has remarkable stuff. On a special occasion—the birthday of one of my children, or our wedding anniversary— I'll bring home a basket of fresh figs, or mulberries, or lychees, or mangosteen, or that truly weird pink-and-green object known as dragon fruit. (Amazing what grows in the land of Israel these days.)

So, as I say, Amalia and I . . .

And no, I haven't the faintest idea why Mr. Fig is called Mr. Fig nor why Mr. Pineapple Mr. Pineapple. That is not something anybody ever needs to think about. Needless to say, Mr. Fig and Mr. Pineapple have always been bitter rivals. . . .

Oh yes, Amalia. I don't really know how to describe her.

There is no word in Hebrew for what she is, what we are, were. Maybe in some foreign language; the language of a peaceful country where minor incidents are the worst and best things that happen.

Amalia and I, it began with fruit and it ended with fruit.

I was in Mr. Fig a little over a year ago, on my way home from work, picking up a few last-minute items. I brought my selection to the counter. There was only one person ahead of me, a ginger-haired woman about my own age, who had already placed her purchases on the counter. I watched while Mr. Fig set each in turn on the scales, calculated the prices of the various items, and the total. Apples, oranges, pears, kiwis, grapefruit. The ceremony of the money being handed over, the change being returned; the redhead shunting the goods into her bag. Interesting enough, in its way. (I imagine television-watching must be a similar experience—there's a whole life implied in these daily necessities.) And I began to set out my own.

I noticed, to one side of the counter, tucked on a shelf beside the bananas, a single basket of strawberries. It did not belong. Strawberries were displayed elsewhere. My instinct, naturally, was to ask the woman, "Excuse me. Is this yours?" But before I said a word, I understood, in a flash, just what the story had been. She had been walking down the aisles, checking her list, choosing what she and her family needed, and suddenly she had been struck by the glorious berries. Expensive, certainly by Mr. Fig's standards, for this was at the very opening of the strawberry season. Yet she had been tempted. She had taken one basket—although she could not really afford it; she knew she shouldn't. She had brought the fruit to the cashier. And then, at the very last minute, she had repented. She had left the strawberries behind on purpose. And were I to go "Excuse me" and offer her own fruit to her, she'd blush—her cheeks would be as red as her hair, as red as the strawberries. . . . So I couldn't resist. How could I have done? And she did indeed blush—she stammered something about not wanting them after all—and I said something to the effect that surely she wouldn't mind if I bought them then? Of course she would not mind.

I abandoned all my other fruit, there at the counter, and took only the strawberries. I ran out after her. I trailed her up the road to the playground by Mendele Street. And we sat on one of the benches—a little distance from the infants romping up ropes and ladders and sliding down chutes—sharing the strawberries between us.

We talked, Amalia and I. What did we talk about? Oh, the usual subjects that strangers are permitted to talk about in Israel . . . Death. Destruction. . . . There was one of those campaigns going on at the time, I forget which . . . Operation Retribution? Operation Grapes of Wrath? . . . some name like that. It didn't concern either of us directly. We were too old to be called up on reserve duty, and our children were too young to fight. But still, it was urgent; we were entitled to have opinions, to agree and to disagree with one another, passionately. . . . And why yes, we did mention my wife and her husband, our children—but only in passing; that was not what it was all about. We promised to get together soon.

This was how it was. Every couple of weeks—no, rarer than that, roughly every month—we'd phone. Either I would call her, or she me. Then we'd arrange to get together. Never in private, no; always in some public place, a café, a restaurant—in the evening, when it is busiest. (There's a privacy one has amidst a crowd.) Either I'd be there first, or she would. And the second person—she or I—would say to the first, "Excuse me. Do you mind if I share your table?" "No, of course not. Please take a seat." And so we would talk, as if we were strangers— which, to be sure, in a way we always were. Intimate strangers was what we aspired to be. We had spouses already, we had friends from way back; what was missing was precisely the closeness of transience. We chatted about politics and war, and so on; nothing too personal. And not infrequently somebody one of us knew would chance by. (Jerusalem is a village, after all.) We'd greet the newcomer. And then introduce the other. "And oh by the way this is . . . I'm sorry, I didn't catch your name." And so it would go on.

Until on Kesarya Street. The Wednesday before the Wednesday before last. An incident . . . We had left the café (pleasant enough; one of the branches of *Aroma*) and we were walking a little way together, until we would have to part (I to my home in Rehavia, she to hers in Talbieh), and we turned onto Kesarya Street, and there it was. We saw the illumination first. Police and fire lights whirling; a kind of klieg light against the building, as if it were being used as a location for a film. A group of twenty or thirty onlookers was gathered already. As we came closer, we saw water streaming down the pavement; asphalt gleamed. The scarlet mass of the fire engine. Amalia swore she glimpsed a red blob of flame, a berry's worth, though personally I think that was sheer imagination (a loose strand of her own hair catching the light?). Me, I saw only smoke.

A wisp of smoke hovering next to Mr. Pineapple—nothing more.

There was no serious damage. There's a juniper tree on the adjacent corner, and I presume this must have smoldered a little, because charred, dampened cones littered the ground. And the man with the fire hose was still at work, aiming his jet up among the boughs of the juniper, just in case there were embers trapped up there that might glow again and set the whole thing ablaze. A couple of paramedics, men in orange jackets and knitted kipas, were idling around, with nothing to do. There were soot marks on the walls; and one of the windows of Mr. Pineapple had been broken, as likely as not by the firefighters, so they could investigate, and aim their hose inside.

We were among the ranks of gawpers on the far side of the street.

There was a journalist with a notebook, asking questions of a policeman. There was one of those TV men with a camera strapped to his body, the way you carry your assault rifle. It seemed he was shifting it effortlessly, as if it were part of his body—but I remembered from my wars: it always weighs next to nothing when you first sling it on; by the end of the day it weighs a ton and your shoulder is aching.

I suppose everybody was thinking what I was thinking, what Amalia must have been thinking. Surely the culprit was . . . But we don't *know* that; and nobody said it out loud. And really it's equally likely to have been just one of those things. An electrical fault, say; or maybe Mr. Pineapple had been trying to warm himself with his ancient Friedmann kerosene heater. . . . And it's not as if anybody had been injured let alone killed. And no doubt the insurance would cover it. So it was with a reasonably good conscience that Amalia and I and all the rest were happy enough to ogle the spectacle as if it had been put on for our benefit—street theater. Though in truth nothing much was happening at this point, just the steady play of the stream of water against the juniper.

We watched the scene until a little after midnight. And then, separately, Amalia and I went home.

To my surprise, when I got back, my wife was still awake. She was lying in bed, staring up at the ceiling.

I undressed rapidly and got into bed beside her. I kissed her on the cheek, as I do every night.

I was silent. What should I have talked about? Even politics has been rather petty and repetitive of late—nothing worth bothering with.

Eventually I said, "Hello, Cinderella."

"Hello *who*?"

She changed the subject. "You remember, dear. We're invited to the Brenners tomorrow?"

"That's right," I said. "They said we should turn up at 8:30, which actually means 9:15. You know the Brenners!"

"Shall we bring a gift?"

"Do you think we should? If you like—?"

"How about fruit?" she said. "You can pick up something at Mr. Pineapple."

"What kind of fruit," I replied carefully, "were you thinking of, dear?"

"Oh, I'll leave it up to you."

She rolled over, facing away from me. She fell asleep.

But I didn't go to sleep, not for a while at any rate. I realized: she must have seen it on television. Local news. The Incident on Kesarya Street . . . And, well, it's not as if Amalia and I

were doing anything, but all the same. . . . How we were standing relative to one another. Our expressions; how the street
lights, the reflections of the klieg light, the redness of the fire
engine, the slowly strobing blue of the police—how all of these
lit us up.

And now what? The Incident happened three weeks ago. I
haven't rung Amalia to arrange another meeting, and she hasn't
rung me. . . . I don't see how we could ever meet up again. It just
wouldn't be possible now. . . . And if I can't see her, then how
ever will I be able to cope?

I often think of what happened at the company I work for.
During the Gulf War, several of the executives and the secre-
taries, half a dozen of either sex, retreated to the sealed room at
the top of the building when the air raid warning began—just
as you were supposed to. (I stayed at home that day.) Twelve
human beings in one confined space. And they remained there
until the All Clear. And meanwhile, naked apart from their gas
masks, they made passionate love. . . . Inevitably, the various
wives and husbands, boyfriends and girlfriends, got to hear of
it. The participants were duly forgiven. It couldn't be more
understandable: Scud missiles are raining down, we all might
die at any minute. . . . What's the worst they could be accused
of, after all? Does anybody think they personally persuaded
Saddam Hussein to invade Kuwait, just so they could have an
orgy? And history's not going to repeat itself, not in the
remotely conceivable future.

Ah, it's so easy to cope with crisis, with danger—when the

sirens blast, we can all be brave and virtuous; or if we're not, we're only human. When the Messiah dies, we can pray he will resurrect himself; and either he will or he won't.... But in a tolerable age, with no Armageddon and no Messiah, when all we have to deal with are "Incidents"—how on earth can we compose our lives?

Love and Coffee

～ **My wife and I are sitting in a coffeehouse, not our usual** coffeehouse, not the coffeehouse we always go to, the one on Bograshov Street near the beach, with the round tables and the square windows, the coffeehouse that's been around forever; no, instead we're at a different coffeehouse, on Dizengoff Street not far from the funny fountain (it's got sprays that go up and down to music): this coffeehouse has also been around forever but somehow we never go to it, all the same here we are, because every married couple is entitled to, needs to, once in a blue moon, make a small change in their life—and besides, we wanted to know if the cappuccinos here are better or worse than the cappuccinos at our regular place. About the same, actually.

When we arrived there were no empty tables, so we asked a man studying a newspaper if we could share his. He waved at the seats. We sat down. Now that my wife and I have sipped about a third of our cappuccinos, and we've said all we have to say about them—we think it's about time we have a conversation with the man. He's not young; he's wearing a hearing aid in his left ear—the kind that's transparent so you're supposed not to notice but actually it makes it all the more visible: it gleams like a jellyfish. And of course that does make it a little awkward. I mean, it's only polite to have a conversation—about politics, for example, or religion—but he hasn't caught our eye, and the last thing we want to do this fine sunny morning is yell at a deaf man.

But then he looks up and smiles at us. He points at the sugar bowl. Actually we don't want any more: we already have enough . . . but isn't it interesting that they don't have cubes of sugar any more: nowadays they have these narrow long paper sachets, specially imported from Italy; half of them have a picture of a lady in a red dress and half of a man in eveningwear, and if you put the two sachets side by side, the man and the woman are dancing—but all the same we think the good old cubes were simpler and less fuss? . . . and he agrees with us: he's on our side, so we do have a conversation going after all.

Then we tell him we don't usually go to this coffeehouse, we usually go to another coffeehouse, and he tells us he always goes to this coffeehouse, he never goes to our coffeehouse, so we suggest now that we've come here he can go there some time, and he says he definitely might.

Next we look at his paper to read the headlines—but he explains there's nothing interesting in it—it's just the same old news; and in fact he hasn't got a whole newspaper, it's just a bit of a newspaper, a couple of pages that somebody had left behind and smeared with honey. The way it works at this coffeehouse is that all the newspapers are put in a heap and people take what they want and put back what they want, which means after an hour or two everything is muddled: Economy from *Ha'aretz* next to Fashion from *Ma'ariv* next to Sports from *Jerusalem Post* next to Classified from *Yediot Aharonot* with inked circles around items of interest next to something we don't know what it is from the Russian newspaper, *Vesty* . . . and we tell him that in our coffeehouse the newspapers are fixed to cleft sticks so they don't fall apart, and isn't that a much better idea? And he says he never reads the newspapers anyway—all lies.

Then we are happy to return to the subject of coffee. What we like. What we don't like. My wife and I find espresso troubles our digestion; he tells us he's never noticed that personally. He likes a dark roast; we like ours medium. He once tried soy milk in his caffe latte, and it wasn't very nice; we've never tried it but we're sure he's right. . . . And we mention interesting coffee experiences we've had in our lives. . . . During our honeymoon in Venice, for instance . . . When he arrived in Jaffa, illegally, in 1946 . . . His speech is quite normal, and provided we speak clearly and make sure he can see our lips, he can understand almost everything we say.

And then there's a little pause, as we're all trying to remember the coffees that have had the greatest impact in our lives . . . and sure enough, we start discussing our army days. Ah! military coffee, there's something about it, the three of us are in complete agreement there. My wife tells a story about a truly delicious cup she had after she'd been up all night, in a communications room on the Syrian border, during the Six

Day War. And at practically the very same moment he'd been drinking coffee in his tank in the Mitla Pass in the Sinai! ... And I chime in with a story of my own—I was ground crew for the bombing sorties over Transjordan—also about the coffee of '67.

Ah, it's the one thing I regret about growing older, now that I'm no longer called up for reserve duty.... There's absolutely nothing like it, when we've been up all night, somewhere in the mountains of the north (or in the desert, the man interrupts), yes the desert can be chilly too, when dawn is breaking, and perhaps we hear the call of the rock sparrow (or a formation of wild ducks flying overhead, my wife says), and in the distance we see the crack troops of the Golani Brigade marching past en route to the front, chanting that chant of theirs, in their uncouth schoolboy voices, *I want to fuck someone right now!* over and over again, how strangely innocent it seems, at that hour ... and then one of our comrades, he's already lit the propane burner, and another comrade, he gets out the packet of Turkish coffee scented with cardamom and he spoons just the right amount, as well as plenty of sugar, into the stainless-steel—whatdyoucallit—a kind of pot, the special kind you make Turkish coffee in—*finjan!* my wife sings out, and at the very moment that her upper teeth arrive on her lower lip, about to make the initial f, I recall it too, and so does the deaf man—*finjan!* we three chorus together; yes ... and we sit there, in the hills, or in the desert, or next to a temporary airstrip somewhere in the Jezreel Valley, rubbing our hands together, our breath steaming in the crisp early morning air ... and finally the coffee boils, the froth rises to the top of the finjan: once, twice, three times, and the froth clears, and a cupful is poured out, one for her, one for him, and one for me, and yes, the grounds get between our teeth, and its aroma is tainted with diesel, but all the same it's the most delicious drink in the whole wide world!

And while I'd been remembering this . . . the deaf man had begun talking. He was already well into his own coffee-related anecdote.

As best as I could gather, the deaf man's story was about a woman called Nehama who worked on the production line at a giant coffee factory, somewhere on the outskirts of Tel Aviv, in an industrial zone to the south. I wasn't clear as to the date of his story, but I somehow got the impression it was set back in the 1960s (though maybe I misunderstood—the period really isn't vital). This factory specialized in supplying coffee to the armed forces. There was a part of the factory where the raw beans were unloaded—straight out of the containers from the ports of Eilat and Ashdod. Another part where the beans were sorted. A part where the beans were roasted (an intoxicating smell there) to varying degrees. And elsewhere the coffee was ground to different degrees of fineness. And the coffee was channeled into a giant machine that packaged it: and the packages were put into boxes, for delivery to the Israel Defense Forces—and it was in this last section that Nehama worked.

Now what she used to do was write poems and slip them inside the coffee packets. Not very good poems, perhaps. The

Whate'er Fate may put you through
Know that somebody loves you!

kind. And she'd sign them: Nehama.

So what happened, of course, was that her poems were read

by brave young soldiers, and sailors, and air force people—and sometimes we're sure they were tossed away, perhaps with some comment about sentimental claptrap; and other times they were appreciated: the fighter would be glad to know that somebody, whoever she was, cared, and then the poem would be disposed of. . . . But every so often the poem would be treasured. A lonely conscript would think: Who could Nehama be, so enchanting and thoughtful? He would fold the poem, and press it into his breast pocket. . . .

And one day a handsome young soldier on leave actually came to the factory in Tel Aviv. He had deduced that the factory must be the source of his poem. He had tracked the location down. . . . So he turned up at the front gate, and he said,

"Does anybody called Nehama work here?"

The security guard shrugged. What does he know? There are many women employed in this factory, and men too. But the soldier was welcome to have a look.

So this young man marched into the factory. He inquired at the unloading yard. He inquired on the sorting floor. He inquired in the roasting unit, and in the grinding zone. . . .

At last he found himself in the big building where the coffee is packaged and prepared for shipping. He stood at the beginning of the long conveyor belt there, that winds to and fro. A smelly black powder is sifted through funnels into a continuous foil-and-plastic tube, which is automatically snipped off and heat-sealed, thus forming a succession of coffee bags. The employees, mostly women, in blue overalls and hairnets and latex gloves, supervise and tend the machines—they identify and dispose of imperfect bags—they check that the bags are filling up the cardboard boxes, as they should—they do all sorts of other tasks that have to be done to keep complicated and expensive packaging machines working properly—and finally they label the boxes and seal them—and let them slide away on the conveyor belt toward the delivery department.

The handsome young soldier comes in.

He stands at the back of the production line.

The employees are too busy to notice him.

He walks all around, not straying far from the conveyor belt, perhaps too shy to ask which of the many workers is Nehama, or perhaps he just wants to prolong the suspense. . . . Eventually he taps one woman on the shoulder.

The woman he has chosen is an older woman with white hairs poking out from under her hairnet, wrinkled and tired. He knows she isn't the woman of his dreams—and maybe that's why he's chosen her. She's standing quite near the bottom of the conveyor belt, where she works during her shift.

"Excuse me," he says. "I wonder if by any chance somebody called Nehama works here."

Now it just so happens, by coincidence, that the person he's addressing is indeed Nehama! Yes, the very one who puts poems into IDF coffee packages.

She is about to open her mouth . . . She sees this handsome young officer, his eyes so full of hope . . . and she replies:

"Nehama. Yes. She did use to work here. But I'm afraid she left . . . No, nobody knows how to contact her now . . . Good luck. I hope you find her."

And as the young man walks away, the old woman's eyes fill with tears. And she reflects that surely, somewhere, in the whole of Israel, some day, he will indeed find his Nehama.

*

The deaf man puts on his hat. He explains he has a place he has to get to, and he thanks us for our conversation.

And actually it's about time for us to go home too. It's almost noon. My wife and I really should have our afternoon nap.

So all three of us stand up . . . I need to use the washroom: I turn to ask the waiter where it is. . . . The deaf man walks ahead, and my wife calls after him. But naturally he doesn't hear, so she has to run and touch him on the shoulder.

"Excuse me," she says. "How did you learn about that story?"

"Oh," he says. "The story took place many years ago. I was the handsome young soldier then."

Well, we don't go back to that coffeehouse on Dizengoff near the funny fountain ever again. There was nothing wrong with it, but once was enough. Instead, every morning we drink cappuccinos at our usual coffeehouse on Bograshov Street near the beach.

And so of course we don't see the deaf man. . . . But we do think about him, my wife and I, and we do wonder about his story.

It was my wife who pointed out the logical flaw:

"If he was the young soldier—then how could he possibly know the whole story? The point is that the soldier never learned who the original Nehama was!"

Of course she is right, but I tried to think of ways in which the soldier could have found out the truth. For example:

"Maybe he then asked somebody else in the factory to point out Nehama?"

And my wife said, "Yes, that might have happened, but if so, then the story wouldn't be very interesting. It's only romantic because he *didn't* know."

And sure enough (Tel Aviv is really quite small—far stranger coincidences have happened) we run into the deaf man a few months later. Well, we don't exactly run into him: we're going for a stroll after our cappuccinos (my wife has reminded me we have to buy a get well card for our daughter-in-law who recently had a hysterectomy) along Ibn Gavirol, and we see him on the opposite side of the road: he's walking and then he reaches a bus stop, and he stands there.

So my wife, she takes me by the arm, and we cross the road illegally (the traffic pauses for us; the drivers are really quite polite) and we arrive at the bus stop just as the deaf man is getting on a bus.

So we wait till he is inside, along with many other people, and we buy our tickets and find seats.

We see him, but he doesn't see us.

"Why are we taking this bus?" I whisper to my wife.

She whispers back, "I'll explain everything later."

. . . And we stay on the bus, past the big open market, past Jaffa, all the way to nearly the end of the line—an industrial suburb in the south.

When we get off, the first thing we notice is the smell of coffee everywhere.

A huge coffee factory dominates the skyline.

The deaf man walks ahead, in through the main entrance.

My wife and I, we go around the side to the loading dock—

forklift trucks are taking out cardboard boxes, marked with shipping labels for the IDF and elsewhere. We climb the steps next to the loading dock, go into a warehouse (we get some funny looks, but nobody stops us), and we keep on walking, through a glass door that says EXIT in mirror image, into the big open area where the coffee is packaged.

It's pretty noisy. The conveyor belt zigzags through the space—like a road that's winding down a steep hill, only all on one level. A hundred workers are laboring at different points. And there's the old man, in his blue work coat and his hairnet, inspecting a stream of coffee packages that are tumbling into a box.

My wife and I, we watch the scene for a while.

Then I go over to one of the women who works here. . . . I cough, and she turns.

She's quite young, with a round clear white face, blue eyes and a pert little snub nose.

"What are you looking for?" she says, in a strong Russian accent.

"Is it true?" I say. "Does the deaf man write little poems, and sign them Nehama, and drop them in the coffee boxes?"

She laughs.

I go on:

"And tell me, has it ever happened that somebody's read one of his poems, and comes here, wanting to meet Nehama?"

She laughs her jolly laugh some more, and says:

"Sure. Every few months we get another. Some man looking for his Nehama."

"And what do you tell him?"

She tilts her head to one side, and gives me an assessing stare.

"That all depends . . . "

By now, several other women have left their posts on the production line and have come over to see what's going on. They are gathered around, listening.

The Russian woman continues: "If the man is old and ugly, we tell him: No, Nehama doesn't work here any more.... But if he's kind and manly, and has beautiful eyes, then we tell him ... "

The Russian woman has slipped her arms around my waist and she is gazing up into my eyes. She moans huskily: "I'm Nehama."

And then another woman hoops her arms around me from behind. "Me! I'm the real Nehama!"

And a third woman presses my hand between both of her latex-gloved ones. "I'm your one and only Nehama."

And here's a fourth woman, and a fifth, a sixth—all of them laughing as they flirt with the stranger in the coffee factory.

"I'm Nehama!"

"I'm the one and only Nehama!"

"I'm the Nehama you've been waiting for!"

And meanwhile the deaf man is working away, with his back to us, his hearing aid shiny as the moon as it catches the fluorescent light....

And at last my wife, Ruth, saunters slowly and elegantly across the concrete factory floor, and she leans through the mass of women clustered about me, and she kisses me gently on the lips.

I say, "Hello, Nehama."

The Chair At the Edge of the Desert

⌇ There was a yellow chair at the edge of the desert. It was made of pine, and had been painted a bright buttercup-yellow long ago. It had been designed as a rocking chair, and, though one of the rockers was cracked and the other was out of true, it did rock by itself on windy days. For all I know, it may be there still. To reach it, you drive out of Dimona along a narrow, badly maintained road that doesn't lead anywhere in particular, except to one of the storage facilities for radioactive waste we aren't supposed to talk about; a dirt track branches off, and there's a rusty broken sign that nobody has bothered to remove: *This Way To Kibbutz*. A few minutes further on, that's where the chair is.

The last time I drove along that road in my truck, I slowed to a crawl and sounded my horn. I passed the turnoff and the sign. I eased almost to a halt in front of the chair. The yellow paint was pitted. A calm day: the chair was scarcely trembling. I released the brake, and accelerated into the desert.

As best as anybody can tell, Yigal had never officially been a member of the kibbutz. He had been there before the birth of the kibbutz; he was still there after its death. He lived in a shack he had built himself out of shipping crates and drainage pipes and agricultural polyethylene; his stove was made from the turret of a Russian-built T-1 tank, wrecked farther south, that had somehow been salvaged and dragged up here. Strictly speaking he was squatting, but since he had long worked for the kibbutz, picking avocados and carnations in their appropriate seasons, and tending the date palms, nobody minded. It is believed that at one point, in July 1967, during the flood of fellow-feeling that spread across the nation after the war, he was actually invited to become a kibbutznik. He refused: he was not the collective sort.

As for the kibbutz—yes it did pass away. It had never been one of the famous or venerable kibbutzim—still, it was around for a few generations: people grew up or grew old here: it can hardly be called a failure. It was established in 1953. Ben Gurion had declared that the desert should bloom—it had seemed a noble cause. The founders had moved down here from other, more successful kibbutzim in the north; they had drawn in immigrants, survivors from Czechoslovakia and Hungary, who were willing to commit to hard work, dry heat, idealism. . . . It had flourished in the '60s. Already by the '70s there was discontent—the younger generation was seduced away to the cities, or even abroad. It was said that the kibbutz was an out-moded way of life. It was said that it deprived its members of an individualist freedom, to which we all are entitled. It was said that, while intending to do good, it ended up doing harm, on balance. . . . It did not survive to the end of the millennium.

Afterwards—after the Movement had officially closed down the kibbutz—after the survivors had moved away, to Beersheba or Dimona or Jerusalem, or, in the case of the handful of committed souls, to a newer, barer, more rigorous kibbutz farther south, near Ovda—nobody was left here, officially. Apart, that is, from Yigal—who had never been official in the first place—and two old women who refused to leave and in any case had nowhere else to go.

Their names were Granny Hannele and Granny Rivki. They had come here as girls. They had fallen in love here; they had married and given birth here (actually only Granny Hannele had; Granny Rivki was merely an honorary "Granny"); they weren't about to set out to seek their fortune elsewhere, not at their time of life. Besides, the government was in the process of being persuaded to buy up the land, for hush-hush purposes, at a price several times the going rate (much string-pulling would be required to bring this about: the Movement would have to call in its favors and use its political connections): when that happened, anybody left here would certainly be evicted. It was of no great importance what took place here meantime.

Yigal looked after the two old women. It has been suggested that he received a lump sum as payment—although no record to this effect has been found in the kibbutz archives. Whether he was a philanthropist or a hireling is beside the point. The fact is, he did feed them, and wash them down once a week or so, and took care of the toilet arrangements as best as anybody could. And he provided them with entertainment—mornings, he guided them to the roadside, where they watched the traffic—every hour or so a Peugeot pickup would drift past, or a crow, or a gecko, or a Toyota Landcruiser . . . by the evenings they were indoors again. They slept in what had been the vegetable packaging shed—the coolest building still in one piece. He shuttled them to and from the roadside in their one wheelchair.

Strictly speaking the wheelchair belonged to Granny Hannele—who was paralyzed from the waist down, as well as being senile. Granny Rivki could walk several steps, with the aid of her stick; and she was observant enough to realize she was being taken somewhere and, often, to object vehemently. It followed that the process of transferring the Grannies was a slow and tricky one.

First Yigal would carry Granny Rivki from her bed, put her into the wheelchair—and take her about ten meters. He would unload her, depositing her on the ground. He would go back for Granny Hannele, take her about ten meters farther than Granny Rivki; and put her on the ground. Then back—pick up Granny Rivki—then back for Granny Hannele—and so on. In the late afternoon, the process would be reversed. The point being that it wasn't safe to let Granny Rivki out of his sight—she might wander off and do herself mischief; and it wasn't possible to transport them simultaneously.

He had tried fitting the two Grannies together on the wheelchair, in different arrangements (one sitting on the other's lap; or Granny Rivki with her arms around Granny Hannele, as if hugging, or wrestling like Jacob and the Angel), fixing them in place with bits of string and wire—but there was simply no way of accomplishing this without causing upset or even injury. And anyway, if the procedure was time-consuming and awkward—it wasn't as if the three of them had anything better to be doing.

Most of the day one of the Grannies would be sat in the rocking chair, and the other in the wheelchair. Yigal would be between them, cross-legged on the pebbly sand. From time to time he would swap them around.

The only person who saw the three of them on a regular basis was the Ethiopian immigrant who drove the truck to the nuclear waste site we're not supposed to talk about. He had an arrangement whereby he'd pick up groceries at the Supersol in Dimona every Thursday, and drop them by the turnoff. Yigal would be waiting there with payment plus a five percent commission. The Ethiopian spoke limited Hebrew; and what was there to discuss? "Here is the receipt." "Here is what I owe you." "Thank you." "Goodbye." Whether this was paid for out of Yigal's own savings or whether it originally came from the kibbutz is not the point: the savings were finite: sooner or later there would be nothing left. The only question is whether the money would run out while the Grannies were still alive. . . .

The one break in the routine was on Saturdays, when Yigal would escort the Grannies beyond the buildings and the fields to the kibbutz graveyard. There lay the mortal remains of about forty kibbutzniks—including Granny Hannele's husband, and two of her children, as well as one grandchild. Also Granny Rivki's beloved. In addition to many others who had once lived and worked in this place. Who had given it so much love and sweat. Who had done what they had to do, day by day. . . . No prayers were said. No traffic was visible or audible in this quiet spot in the shade of the date palms. . . .

As to why Yigal cared so religiously for these two old ladies—there is no knowing. Perhaps it was simply that he could not think what else to do with them. Those who call him a saint are no doubt exaggerating.

One hot morning in winter Yigal had taken the Grannies to the roadside, and he was feeding them their breakfast. For Granny Rivki, matza dipped in leben and tehina. Toothless, she was chewing it with her gums, not hard but thoroughly. Granny Hannele needed to have the food dampened first, then spooned carefully into her mouth. Now and again he would give them sips of water.

While eating, Granny Rivki fell asleep in the rocking chair. She snored with her mouth open, bits of the meal visible on her palate and tongue. Meanwhile Granny Hannele gave a little meow, and she vomited what she had eaten—an off-white gruel dribbling down her chin and neck.

Yigal set off back to his own shack to fetch an old newspaper and extra water, to clean her up.

He couldn't have been gone more than a minute.

When he came back, he saw the empty yellow chair. He saw Granny Rivki, on hands and knees, crawling across the road. He saw an eighteen-wheeler go roaring by—possibly the driver was aware of nothing. Granny Rivki was thrown by the impact into the drainage ditch beside the road. A purple bruise on her forehead. The yellow chair kept rocking in the wind from the vehicle that had passed by.

There was no question that Granny Rivki was dead. Yigal let her slump back on the ground. He went and cleaned up Granny Hannele, as he had intended, since after all Granny Rivki could wait a while.

Then Granny Hannele in turn fell asleep. He pulled her bonnet forward to shade her head.

What now should he do about the body?

Although he didn't believe in reporting anything to the authorities—he was hardly in a position to bury Granny Rivki himself, not properly at least so that no wild creature could dig her up. There seemed no alternative. He would have to get a lift into Dimona, him along with the two Grannies—the live one and the dead one—and sort things out there. . . .

He stood by the roadside, his right arm stuck out, the hand pointing down, in standard hitchhiker posture—although there was no traffic to be seen or heard. Then, almost an hour later, when a Jeep in desert camouflage came speeding along, jolting from side to side, Yigal jumped in the air waving his arms up and down vigorously, as if communicating in frantic semaphore or hailing an unexpected triumph.

The Jeep skidded to a halt. The driver—a young fellow, hardly old enough to be driving, it seemed, in army uniform with a corporal's stripe—jumped out.

Yigal, exhausted from his efforts, could only point.

The soldier looked aghast. The living Granny. The empty chair. The corpse on the ground.

"I didn't do it!" he shrieked. "It wasn't my fault! I swear!"

He opened his wallet and thrust the contents—about three

hundred shekels and a Bezeq telephone card—into Yigal's hands.

"You never saw me! It wasn't me!"

He jumped back into his jeep and, swerving in a screeching U-turn, disappeared the way he had come.

Yigal clambered into the drainage ditch. He settled down on top of some dry leaves, dry sticks, and an empty Maccabee beer can. He fell into a deep sleep. . . .

When he woke up, it was nearly dusk.

"Granny Rivki? Granny Hannele?" he called softly.

Then he remembered what had happened that morning.

He checked the corpse—which was indeed still dead. . . . So it had not been a dream.

He rose, silhouetted against the beautiful red sunset, and began scything his arms in the air. . . .

As if miraculously, a rented Nissan containing two lost Swedish tourists came trundling along the road from Dimona. The car stopped. The Swedes were blondes wearing bikinis. Both got out, and followed Yigal's gaze to the dead old woman.

"Oh my God!" they screamed in English; also something in what was presumably their mother tongue.

They pushed some colorful banknotes, of inestimable value, into Yigal's hands.

Then they drove away into the dark, down the road that goes somewhere they almost certainly did not mean to go.

The following morning, Yigal added to his savings with a contribution from the driver of the Angel Bakery van, and another from that of a Harley-Davidson. . . . He was not greedy. In any case, it would have been neither respectful nor prudent to put Granny Rivki out to earn her keep in the heat of the day.

There was a propane-powered refrigerator-room behind what had been the kitchen (where perishables had once been stored; also carnations had been cooled here, for longer shelf-life). With some effort (he had to poke the remains of a scorpion from one of the pipes) he managed to get the refrigeration system working again.

He let Granny Hannele lie abed for once.

Back at the roadside he collected Granny Rivki with the wheelchair (rigor mortis meant he had to balance her across the chair arms, tying her in place) and brought her to the refrigerator-room.

After lunch, he examined her again. Her bruise was not quite as prominent as it might be. . . . He found a lipstick in her handbag, and—what with a little Nescafé to darken it, plus dirt—he managed to give her a more realistic wound.

About five o'clock, when it wasn't quite so hot, he brought Granny Rivki back to her appointed place, on the wrong side of the white line on the asphalt. He wheeled Granny Hannele down to accompany him.

He sat in the yellow rocking chair himself, and waited for the next vehicle to happen by.

This went on for six days. It wasn't easy to tell, but Granny Hannele seemed to enjoy having traffic accelerate and decelerate near her—the shrieking—the profanities—the oaths: "in God's name" and "on my mother's life!". . . As for Granny Rivki, it obviously made no difference to her. (The Ethiopian dropped off the groceries on his usual Thursday; but he claimed to have observed nothing.) And Yigal, for the first time in his life, had found a steady, reliable source of income, in which he had to interact on a daily basis with other human beings, of varying dispositions. Surely it was good for him. You might reasonably suppose that he was at long last growing up. . . .

Until on the seventh day, in the afternoon, an unloaded flat-top truck rolled at a gentle pace down the road from the nuclear waste site.

The truck braked.

The driver stepped out.

He stood beside Granny Rivki. He lowered his head. There was a moment of silence. Then he crouched down, and he whispered to her, "You have nothing to worry about. Death is not a thing *in* life."

He spoke to Yigal.

"Of course I'll take the body to the mortuary in Dimona. Was she a friend or relative of yours?"

"I've never seen her before in my life."

"Or of yours?" he asked Granny Hannele in the wheelchair.

She smiled and said nothing.

The driver single-handedly bore the light, fragile corpse onto the back of his truck. He climbed into the cab and drove carefully away toward the town.

Now at last Yigal was free to mourn. "Granny!" he cried several times—disturbing Granny Hannele, who seemed to look at him with an air of comprehension.

He shook his fist after the departing truck.

"Thief! Slanderer! Murderer! Antisemite!"

He wept bitter tears.

Then he took Granny Hannele home, as usual. Changed her,

as usual. Put her to bed, as usual. And went to his own bed, as usual.

The following morning he wheeled Granny Hannele back to the road. This time, however, he did not let her sit in peace. No, instead he laid her down in the very middle of the road, athwart the dividing line.

He returned to the yellow chair—but did not sit. . . .

He went and brought a spade from his shack.

He heaved dry earth on Granny Hannele, just a thin layer, from the feet to the neck; and shook extra over her wig and bonnet—sufficient to camouflage her against the rutted road.

She seemed to be sleeping, with one eye open and one eye closed.

He looked down at her. He panted for a while.

Then, a little tired from his efforts, but satisfied—he took the place of honor in the yellow chair. He waited for what would happen. He rocked to and fro. There was really nothing else for him to do.

Shabah

‿: **The first thing they want is a chair. "Have you got a chair?"**
they ask timidly, in their broken Hebrew. "Have I got a chair!"
I reply, patting them on the elbow. I lead them into the warehouse. Past hundreds of chairs, maybe thousands—straight-
back chairs, armchairs, rocking chairs, deck chairs, swivel chairs,
commodes, stools, love seats . . . every shape and size of chair, in
pretty much every color that any normal person would want
. . . chairs that are brand new, never sat upon, and other chairs
that are in reasonable condition; absolutely no chairs that aren't
sittable on: we mend them, and scrape them down, and repaint
them and reupholster them. . . . And some of the newcomers—
this might surprise you—they're really quite fussy: no, that
chair won't do for me, it's too big; and that chair is too small. . . .
"But this chair!" I say, running over to touch one (I've

developed quite an intuition when it comes to chairs), "This chair is just right!"

Then the newcomer, he puts his arms around the chair, lifts it up, hugging it to himself . . . and he takes it back to wherever he's being housed on a temporary basis—maybe just a room somewhere, a bare room . . . and he puts his chair bang in the middle of that room, and he sits down on it . . . and now at last he's beginning to feel he belongs here, in what he promised himself would be a Promised Land.

Yes, I get to think a lot about chairs. That's how it is, in my job, working for the Charity. These newcomers from the former Soviet Union, from Ethiopia; they're used to different kinds of chairs; they're not easily pleased, I have to persuade them. And not just chairs of course—I do beds, TVs, washing machines, you name it. But I always begin with the chair. If the immigrant feels happy about a chair, the rest will follow.

And where do we get the chairs from? Oh, sometimes people dump them outside their apartment buildings—we drive around in an old army truck and pick them up. Sometimes they're abandoned, just lying there in the middle of the road or along the roadside. Sometimes well-wishers bring them to our door, saving us the trouble. Sometimes we get word of a surplus of chairs at a factory; or a shipment of slightly imperfect chairs that we can fix up. You never really know where the next chair is coming from. And sometimes the chairs are worn, broken down, and I say to myself: maybe we should just burn this one? But, you know—not everybody understands this—with a bit of effort and hard work, just about any chair can be young again.

A good chair's not easy to find. We have strangers—not new immigrants, immigrants who've been here for years, some who were even born here—they come round and beg us for a chair. "Oh go on," they say, "one chair won't hurt." But I have to put my foot down. "I'm sorry. Our chairs are reserved for newcomers only. Why don't you try a yard sale or a department store?"

Chairs—I always treat them with respect. The story of our life begins at the beginning and ends at the end. But a chair—who sat on your chair before you sat on it? And who will sit on it after you sit on it?—A chair's story zigzags about in space and time. . . . Ah, if only chairs could talk!

I was listening to the radio today about *shabah*. They're not allowed to do it any more. The Supreme Court said no. At least that's what the voice on the radio said the Supreme Court said. What it is, there's an interrogator, and he has a suspect (who's a terrorist or maybe he's not actually a terrorist; an informant is what they might call it). So the interrogator, he decides to torture the informant only he tells himself he's not really torturing the informant but actually he is. He makes the informant sit on a chair, a small chair, child-size, uncomfortable, and he straps him in so he can't move, and it hurts like hell until the informant confesses.

So I've been asking myself about the interrogator, what kind of man he must be. Because every morning on the bus to work I think about today's chairs, and then I work with chairs, and sometimes I'll admit I even have little conversations with my chairs, and in the evening I go home, and in the night I dream about chairs and what does *he* dream about? And sometimes I think about the informant, also. But above all I wonder about the chair. The innocent chair. Where does it come from? Where does it go, after it's been used?

Now the interrogator, the *shabah*-man, he's just an ordinary person, probably wears Wranglers, Reeboks, you can walk past him on the street and you never notice him, he has on a black sweater, he's a touch overweight, a permanent frown like he has a headache from last night. . . . He drives down to the shopping mall, the Kanion—he parks—he strides in—and he hurries (jogging his way up two escalators; actually it'd work out quicker to wait for the elevator, but he's impatient) to the largest department store's furniture section.

"Can I help you?" That's the assistant talking. A middle-aged woman, I should think, bottle-blonde, dreaming about Mr. Zakheim who works in accounts. So the interrogator, he doesn't beat about the bush. "Give me a chair, child-size!" And she explains that children's furniture is actually on a higher floor, next to toys. So he has to go up another escalator.

He gets out and he tries again.

"Excuse me, sir?" A different assistant. This one has a Moroccan look, he's bored by his job naturally but thinking of the commission, neat clothing, his head closely shaven, something about his manner suggests he might be gay. "Excuse me. What are you looking for?" Then the interrogator makes his demand—and the assistant, he does his usual smiling as he guides the customer over. "Yes, we do have some excellent chairs, ergonomically designed to suit the body of the growing child." The interrogator barks, "No! Give me the other kind!"

Nevertheless the assistant asks a few polite questions, the ones he always asks, about how old the child is, whether it's a boy or a girl. . . . "Who cares? What the fuck's the difference between a boy's bottom and a girl's bottom, in *your* experience?" The assistant puts on a rigid grin. "Girls like pink."

Meanwhile, in my workshop, I'm turning a secondhand chair upside-down, tugging a leg to see if it wobbles, scraping off a bit of chewing gum stuck to the underside.

And the interrogator and the assistant, they're deep into their chair discussion, or call it an argument, or even a verbal fight. The assistant, he wants his commission, that's all he's thinking about, so he's got to make a sale, he's got to, as they say, "close." As for the interrogator, he really doesn't want to buy any chair from this man, but he knows if he doesn't get the chair here he'll have to get it somewhere else so he's reluctantly worming his way round to letting himself be talked into a chair. Here comes the assistant, shunting forward different chairs, caressing the seat and back. "Look how soft! And washable too!" A few seconds later the interrogator is actually sitting down in a chair (there's no other way to check it out), contorting himself, twisting his body the way the informant will have to, with the right leg stuck up over the left thigh and the right arm spread over the left shoulder.

And I'm putting a couple of matchsticks into the leg-hole, and screwing the leg back in, so it'll fit more snugly.

And the interrogator's testing a different chair, a pink one this time, with his left leg and left arm raised.

Music helps. My radio's on. Some jaunty pop tune that's good to hum, or whistle, or even (why not?) sing along with. Then it turns into a nostalgic sad–happy folk song that we sang in the Six Day War when we all were young. I turn the chair rightside-up, and give it a good shake, and sit down on it myself. Yes . . . steady as a rock.

"Sir, is the chair comfortable?" the assistant inquires. The interrogator's idea of a joke: "I think so. It hasn't complained." No, no! Fair enough for children or dwarfs maybe, but he can't bring himself to buy it. . . . Though he knows he shouldn't, or maybe he somehow doesn't know he shouldn't, he storms past the assistant, and runs down the three flights of escalators, and out through the air-conditioned atrium and into the parking garage. Back in his Subaru sedan—that little mobile room where he feels most at home—he wipes his brow with the back of a hairy hand. The key turns in the ignition.

There's nothing wrong that a lick of paint won't cover up. I spread an old newspaper on the floor to catch the drip. Interviews with politicians and actresses and athletes. I stroke on the off-white gloss, swishing the brush-tip, making sure I slide the paint in all the funny places, between the fingers of the chair, so to speak, and in its armpits and groin. . . . A phone-in on the radio, which I'm not really listening to . . . Off-white blobs on the headlines . . . The thing to do is let it dry.

On the second floor of an apartment building in the suburbs, a husband is stumbling into his own home. It's quite early in the afternoon. He should still be at work. The wife knows better than to ask any questions. She brings him a cup of Turkish coffee spiced with cardamom, the way he likes it, without needing to be told. He is panting; he could stand to lose a few kilos. His jeans sag; there's a gap between the belt and the hem of the black sweater. He gulps the steaming coffee down. The wife reaches up to massage her husband's forehead, but he writhes free, swats her hand away. Meanwhile a child, a boy, about seven or eight or six, is sprawled on a cushion on the floor, watching a cartoon on TV. The man walks—or you might say falls—through a door on the right, and comes out in triumph, carrying a bulky object awkwardly.

"Hey, Dad, what are you doing?"

"What does it look like I'm doing?"

"That's my chair."

"It's mine now."

"It's mine."

"You're too old for it."

"No I'm not."

"Yes you are!"

"No I'm not!"

"It's a chair for little boys! I'm confiscating it!"

The father takes control of the chair, locking his arms around its back, levering it higher, making the chair charge forward like a bull. The son, he lunges up, trying to grab the chair by its horns—by its legs, that is. The father has the advantage: he shakes and pushes, forcing his son to let go, driving him off.

"It's mine," the boy keeps whining, though he knows he's lost. While the father, flushed, sweaty, secure in the knowledge he has taught his son an important lesson and on top of that has won the contest, goes, "What are you? A baby!" Till at last the boy sneaks off to his own room, with the mother shouting after him, "We'll buy you a computer game." And the father—still clutching the chair, not letting it go—shakes his head, "I can't think what's gotten into the boy."

"I hate you, Daddy! I hate you, I hate you!"

I touch the seat of the chair gently; it is dry.

Time to twist the knob, switching off the news. Time to tidy up. Time to put away. Time for the new-old chair to travel across the yard and into the vast high warehouse belonging to the Charity and along past tables and bookshelves and wardrobes and chests-of-drawers, and to settle into its proper place, somewhere near the middle of a row of a hundred other child-size chairs.

And at some point in the future or past or present a family of immigrants from Kyrgyzstan arrives. A father, a mother, also a girl about seven years old. "We want a chair," they say, in their broken Hebrew. And I lead them to the one chair that I think will be just right for them (the girl tests it; she sits on the clean creamy-white seat as on a throne: she is happy with it), that they will put in the middle of their bare apartment, that will be their new beginning.

The Camel-Hair Coat

I'm back doing my reserve duty, and here's my old buddy—hair a bit thinner, belly a bit bigger, an extra wrinkle or two on his forehead, eyelids a bit droopier—and he's wearing a camel-hair coat over his army uniform.

So we give each other high-fives, and he asks after my wife and kids, and I ask after his son, and if he's still in touch with his ex.

And we swap stories about our days together, during our military service.... It was terrible. It was during the original Intifada. They sent us to Gaza.... But thinking back, you know, we had some wild times. You've got to laugh.

And I ask if he knows what's going on. Are we going to be stationed somewhere? What are they going to give us to do? And he says he doesn't know either.

And then I say—"What's with the coat? You're modeling this season's evening wear for the Israel Defense Forces?"

"You don't think it suits me, Yonatan?"

"To be absolutely honest, Ya'ir, no."

And he laughs and he says—"Haven't you heard? I'm now an internet millionaire!"

"You're a what?"

"No it's true, I swear. This venture capital company in Silicon Valley, they found me out. Then they faxed me the ticket, business class, all the way from Tel Aviv to San Jose. And I was picked up at the airport in a stretch limo, no kidding, pure lily-white like I was a virgin bride. And they took me to their office on Sand Hill Road. They shook my hand: *It's a pleasure to do business with you.* And now I'm a, well . . . "

He slaps my knee as he laughs.

"Me, an internet millionaire! Whoever would've thought it?"

I say, "Hey, last year, doing our reserves, you told me you were in the forklift-truck rental business?"

"Well now I'm in the forklift-truck rental internet business. . . . And you, Yonatan, what are you doing?"

"You know . . . "

"Still the same old thing?"

"Still the same old thing."

"Not much money in it, huh?"

"It comes and it goes."

"The amount you earn, you might as well be in the army! And then I went to the Stanford Shopping Center. . . ."

"What?"

"Shopping Center. Shopping like in 'shopping.' Center like in 'center.' Have you heard of it? It's an exclusive mall."

I shake my head.

"Well they have very expensive shops there. One called Nordstrom. And I bought this coat."

He stands up, right there in the barracks, and gives a twirl.

I click my tongue.

"You know, Ya'ir, I don't think this coat is going to be very comfy, not when you're doing training exercises in the heat of the day."

"I'm not going to be wearing it in the heat of the day."

"And you're a perfect sniper target if they really put us on active service."

"Who said anything about active service?"

He takes it off. Lays it down on his bed. Smoothes out the fabric. He folds the arms over, crossing them. Carefully, starting at the bottom, he begins to roll the coat up. . . .

"So tell me, Ya'ir. How does it feel?"

"Being an internet millionaire? Oh, I'm still the same Ya'ir. I'll stand by my old friends."

"No, I meant the coat."

"Well, you know, with a coat like this, a special coat, the kind of coat we internet millionaires wear . . . comfort is not the point."

"So you're saying it's not comfortable? A little too heavy? A little ticklish, maybe, around the collar?"

"What I'm saying, Yonatan, is that we've gone beyond the tired old categories of comfort and ticklishness."

I nod. "Well, I guess you have to suffer to be rich."

He stuffs the rolled coat into his kitbag. He zips the kitbag up.

*

That night I'm on the top and he's on the bottom bunk bed. The lights have just been turned out.

I whisper—"So tell me, Ya'ir. Is it made from real camel hair?"

"You know, if I might say so, for a humble reservist in the IDF, Yonatan, you ask too many questions."

The next morning, at the crack of dawn, they give us a cup of coffee and a bite. Then we're out on a run. . . .

I mean, let's face it. We have office jobs, most of us. We sit at our desks all day long. We're out of condition. We have paunches, mortgages, varicose veins, alimony. . . . We're not teenage athletes anymore. And it's hard to accept some snip of a sergeant, who doesn't look old enough to chew his own gum, screaming orders at us. We can't take this army business seriously.

We run around the perimeter of the base. Then they make us head into the hills—over dry limestone, around shrubs and bushes; a scent of rosemary everywhere; geckos and scorpions scattering for cover. It's uphill almost all of the way. I feel like I'm about to die. . . .

All the same, I don't want to be the first to give up.

Ya'ir pants at me—"Go on, you can do it, Yonatan!"

I pant back—"You can do it, Ya'ir!"

"Easy for *you* to say!"

. . . And afterward, sitting near each other on a rock in the shade of a pine tree, I hum the opening bar of HaTikvah—"*And the anthem is now playing as the gold medalist from Israel in the ten thousand meters, Ya'ir—*"

"Hey, give me a break! Just because I'm an internet million-aire, it doesn't mean I'm perfect in absolutely every way. I can let other people come ahead of me sometimes."

"Well, at least you finished the course."

"You finished too."

"An achievement, at our age . . . "

"It's something."

After lunch, we are given a lecture. Updates on weaponry and communications technology. At least this involves sitting down on chairs, watching and listening. Something we still know how to do.

Then we are supposed to meet with our commanding offi-cer, who will finally reveal the overall plan, what the army intends to do with us; but he relays a message to say he can't make it.

So instead (my theory is they just don't know what to do with us for a couple of hours) they send us over for bayonet practice.

A row of sandbags hung from chains. Crude heads inked on them—mouths and eyes only. Plus a little conventional heart-shape, just about where the heart would really be. The instruc-tor's some scowling girl doing her service. She'll take no shit from any man.

She shouts at everybody:

"Harder!"

"Go straight for the belly!"

"Harder!"

"Silence! You there! Silence! This is serious!"

"Your life and the life of your comrades may well depend on this!"

"You hate that sandbag!"

"You hate it!"

"Yell at the target!"

Ya'ir whispers to me—"Why should I hate it? What's the sandbag ever done to me?"

I whisper back—"You don't want to know."

"What should we yell, Yonatan?"

"Pretend it's our favorite basketball team."

So me and Ya'ir, side by side, our bayonets fixed on our assault rifles, we come running toward our respective sandbags, yelling—"Go go go, Maccabee Tel Aviv!"

That evening, we're tired and achy, of course. Ya'ir wraps his camel-hair coat around him. . . . I show him baby photos: my youngest having her bath. . . . And we put on a cassette of nostalgic music, from the dear old 1980s when the Intifada was in full swing, when we were drafted together, when he got concussed at the Netzarim Junction and I got shrapnel (friendly fire) in my thigh that's still in there, when we were young. . . .

And meanwhile somebody's slipped a sheet of photocopied instructions under the door. Everybody else in the barracks gets to read it; and finally, a little crumpled, it gets passed on to me and Ya'ir.

The deal is as follows. The next day, we'll be training hard. And the day after that, in fact for all the rest of our reserve duty, we'll be posted up north, taking part in a full-scale exercise involving armored units. We'll be expected to play our role in a Syrian Pita Formation.

"What's a Syrian Pita Formation?"

"Beats me, Yonatan."

"I know it was something they taught us, years ago. . . ."

"Yeah. I remember it was something I used to know what it meant. . . ."

"Oh, we can cope. I mean, it's not like they're sending us back to Gaza."

"My God, I hope they don't expect us to fight in a real war."

I tuck away my family snapshots. He puts away his camel-hair coat. Somebody turns off the music. . . .

Bedtime . . . I listen to my old friend's snoring awhile. . . . I drift into a dreamless sleep.

So we're up again early. I mean *really* early, about 3 a.m. One of those surprise wake-ups, just to remind us how glad we are we're not doing our military service anymore. The wide-awake sergeant comes trotting through the barracks, his boots drumming on the floorboards.

"Hey, boys! Egyptian tanks are rolling through Tel Aviv! Jordanian troops are assaulting the Temple Mount! Palestinian troops have captured a falafel stand in Ramat HaSharon! How come you lazy bastards are still in bed?"

They make us do a nighttime cross-country run. . . .

Then back to bed again . . . Sleep till noon.

Lunch. The famous IDF schnitzel made from recycled tank treads.

*

And we spend the afternoon at the firing range. It's quite high-tech: electronic scoreboards tell you how you're doing, and they even offer tips on how you can improve.

I do about as well as can be expected.

But Ya'ir, he scores 34 out of a possible 38.

Back at barracks, he says to me—"Yeah, I guess I'm the same old Ya'ir. Eagle eyes. Steady hands . . . "

"Just luck . . . "

"Yeah. Luck is what a man in my position's got to have. . . ."

"I happen to remember you hardly ever scored so high back then."

"Well what that goes to prove, Yonatan, is that obviously I'm the type who matures, who improves with age, like a fine wine."

We are sitting side by side on my bed.

A thought strikes him.—"Can I borrow your cellphone?"

"Of course. What's wrong with yours?"

"I don't know. The battery's dead, or something. . . . "

I lend him my Pelephone. He taps lots of digits on it; then he starts speaking in English.

"Ya'ir? I hope this isn't an international call? If you're dialing some sex phone line in California, you're going to have to pay me back."

"Shhh. . . ." He presses his finger over his left ear, to drown out my voice and other background noise.

"I'll pay you back, Yonatan. I'll pay everybody back. . . ."

He talks a little more, in English. Then he listens for a while, just grunting from time to time.

He switches the phone off, and hands it back to me.

"What is it, Ya'ir?"

"The stock price has fallen."

"So?"

"So I'm not a millionaire anymore. Does that make you happy? All I have is stock options. If it's selling below the buying price, then I don't have anything."

"And that's bad news?"

"Very bad."

"And maybe tomorrow the stock will rise again?"

"Maybe."

"So who needs to be an internet millionaire anyway?"

"Who?"

"You have good friends, memories, the sun is shining. . . ."

"Sure."

"And who's got time to think about such things? Tomorrow we're all going to be in a Syrian Pita Formation, whatever that is. Maybe they serve hummus with it, on the side?"

"Right."

Then Ya'ir walks over and picks up a wooden chair. He carries it into the yard outside.

He returns and unzips his kitbag. Lifts up the coat like a sleeping child. He carries that outside too, and he drapes it carefully over the back of the chair.

He strides across the yard.

He re-enters the barracks. He fetches his rifle from where he had left it on his bed.

He leans against the doorjamb sideways on, so as to present as narrow a target as possible, in the urban warfare posture they taught us in the old days.

A breeze raises the hair across the coat's back and arms.

The safety on Ya'ir's rifle clicks. . . .

A single shot, and the camel-hair coat is dead.

Spleen; Or, the Goy's Tale

‿∴ I am in the Suq al-Attarin in the Christian Quarter of the Old City seeking to obtain what I do not know the word for. There is a helpful Hebrew translation appended to the street sign; if it is to be believed, Suq al-Attarin translates as Souk of the Perfumers. I sniff long and hard. Not most people's taste in perfume, I should think. A short stocky man in Levis and a Chicago Bulls T-shirt, not too bloodstained, is staring quizzically at me. *"I do not speak Arabic,"* I tell him in Arabic—my one phrase. He replies with his one phrase of Hebrew: *"I do not speak Hebrew."* Then he lifts up a knotted leather strap, and sets about thrashing the air. Flies scoot away from him and take to circling my head instead.

Meat. This is what I intend to buy from the shopkeeper. It will all have to be done by means of sign language—gestures—

a universal language underlying language. He is very good at it. I'm sure he's done it before, often. Bits of meat look like bits of meat—at least they do to me; how can one identify which beast they came from? First he points at a particular joint: he bellows like an ox. Then a different chunk: he frisks about in his Adidas like a baby lamb. Next he snuffles with a goatish expression on his face. Finally he oink-oinks, while curling his littlest finger next to his rump.

There is more to it than this. Now he will show me which part of the animal each piece corresponds to. He taps the meat, then himself. Easy enough to signify the shoulder or the leg thus; but where exactly is the liver, the lungs, or the sweet-breads? My God, one needs an advanced degree in anatomy simply to buy one's lunch!

Our charade has drawn a crowd into the narrow alley, eager to observe the antics. Housewives with shopping bags; idling Greek priests; Palestinian grandmothers in elaborately embroi-dered robes; curious infants. I should explain: I am wearing a black hat, black coat, beard and sidecurls. It cannot be often that they see a rabbi going shopping for nonkosher meat in the Christian Quarter of Jerusalem.

And the funny thing is, I'm actually vegetarian.

Not out of compassion for the poor suffering farm animals. Not for environmental reasons. Not because I'm worried about unhygienic abattoirs, or my cholesterol level. No, it is because of what our sages teach us. The act of eating is a mystical expe-rience. There are sparks of life in everything, and in the process of eating they are transmuted from one essence to another. To eat a carrot or a baked potato is profound enough, in all truth. But to actually consume a leg of chicken or a smoked salmon sandwich! How dare I? In the time of the temple, sacrifice of animals was the primary form of worship. But now, in these degenerate days, who can aspire to possess such piety and chutzpah?

The stone is so awed by the presence of God that it cannot speak. Plants, a higher life-form, are a little further from God's intimate presence. Animals, higher and further. And us, humans, we are so far removed from the Divine Spirit that we gab away at the slightest opportunity, piling story upon story.

And as to why I am buying this meat, this day of all days? Ah, you see, I am a rabbi but, currently, not a Jewish one. Another small story must be inserted at this point. My great-grandmother, born Elena Wyshnedgradsky of Kasimierz, passed away yesterday. And on her deathbed she confessed to me she had come into this world as a Christian. She had converted, of course, when she married my great-grandfather: but her conversion was carried out by a so-called "Reform" rabbi specially imported from Germany, and thus was of no validity in the eyes of God. And since she was my mother's mother's mother, and Jewish identity is passed in the strict maternal line, it follows that I am not now and never have been a Jew.

Naturally I made an emergency call to the rabbinate. I will officially be converted on Tuesday. In accordance with tradition, three times I will be persuaded not to bother—who wants to be a Jew? all those finicky commandments to keep? all that grief?—and three times I will assert my determination notwithstanding. Finally I will receive a token circumcision (a tiny nick with a supersharp razor; one droplet of blood will ooze), a blessing will be said . . . and I'll be back where I supposed myself to have been yesterday morning.

But meantime...If I'm going to be a goy, I may as well do it properly. And the one thing we all know about goyim is that they consume their strange meats, qualmlessly, whenever the desire strikes them, with relish. And I ask myself what stories goyim tell. Certainly they must have stories—for it is in the nature of the human condition—but since they have no shape to their lives, since they are defined in terms of what they are not, how can their stories ever lead anywhere? The stories must begin as a cow and turn into a thistle and then a lump of dirt, an earthworm, a corpse, a human eating a slice of roast beef ...beginnings that are also middles and endings...enough, already!

As I pause in the Suq, trying to make my mind up—a youngish man, a red-and-white keffiya around his neck, murmurs to me in Hebrew:

"Excuse me?"

"You speak Hebrew!"

"Certainly. Also English, also French. I am a polyglot with an excellent knowledge of butchery. Allow me to assist you."

"My pleasure."

We introduce ourselves. His name is Ahmed.

"In former times I was sous-chef at the Four Seasons in Tripoli. Then I became personal chef to Abu Amr—that is, the man you know as Yasir Arafat."

"But you don't work for him anymore?"

"Today I am at your service."

He gives a shrug so magniloquent one could almost think he was Jewish. He launches into an elaborate tale—a succession of self-justifications—something to the effect that Fate has been toying with him, lifting him to dizzy heights and dropping him down again, and he had been fired for overspicing the chicken.

Naturally I pay little attention to the Arab's autobiography. I remind him of his promise to help me.

He turns his attention to the meat display. For my benefit, he translates the various portions of meat.

"And which do you recommend?" I ask. "I seem to remember reading something about Arabs liking sheep's eyeballs. . . ."

"You musn't believe everything you read in books," he advises me. "The most delicious? I should say, the brain or the spleen. A yielding yet firm texture. A concentrated nourishment."

He points at two big blobs of bloody matter.

"You Jews, you boast about brain . . . but I think the spleen is what you secretly prefer. Of course you have to cook it just right."

Ahmed barks instructions to the butcher. Who selects and hacks off for me a couple of kilos of ox spleen.

I hand over what seems a very reasonable sum.

I pat myself down, making sure I still have everything: wallet, handkerchief, revolver, Book of Psalms . . .

Meanwhile the butcher tears some sheets of old newspaper off a hook—a journal in Arabic—which he replaces, at Ahmed's insistence, with an editorial in English. He wraps the meat in this.

"The *International Herald Tribune*," Ahmed informs me. "It is famous for its absorbency."

And finally the butcher drops the purchase into a bag made of skimpy pink plastic. I take it from him. The meat is pleasantly rounded within the see-through pink. . . . Certain forbidden thoughts drift through my mind . . . I banish them by blowing away the flies, and shaking my head, so whisking them with my beard.

I stride back to David Street, and head through the Old City toward Jaffa Gate. The Christians here do not seem surprised to see a Jew carrying a heavy bloody parcel, dripping somewhat—no doubt they have seen it all before, or think they have . . . Ahmed is trailing after me.

"Ahmed," I say. "Now that's a Muslim name, isn't it?"

"Oh, I am beyond all that. I'm an atheist."

"Really? Yes, I think I have heard about you people. . . . What exactly do you atheists do? Do you gather in your atheist congregations? Do you recite atheist doctrines together?"

"We do nothing at all."

"Ah, that must take a great deal of effort."

When we come to the Gate, Ahmed helpfully offers to carry the meat for me.

Now, as we go up Jaffa Road, he walks ahead, him and his bloody load. A familiar enough sight perhaps; the Jews here pay no particular attention to him.

We make conversation. I talk about God and myself.

I ask him where he lives. He tells me he now lives in the Old City, illegally, but he was brought up in a village in Samaria.

"What a coincidence!" I say. "I live just a few kilometers from there." I name my settlement.

He tells me his parents and grandparents still live in the old village.

"Would you like a lift?" I ask, as we reach my VW, parked at the corner of Rabbi Kook Street and The Street of the

Prophets. "I could drop you nearby. We goyim must stick together."

So I get in the driving seat. The spleen takes up the passenger seat. Ahmed sits behind, leaning forward, his chin jutting between the meat and me.

As we drive out of Jerusalem, I ask him for advice on how to cook the meat.

He tells me a recipe. . . . "Mmm-hmm," he concludes, kissing his fingers. It is something with many ingredients: sumac and hyssop and mallow . . . subjected to a complex process involving a succession of bastings and roastings and stewings.

Oddly enough, I cannot memorize his recipe—although I do have an excellent memory when it comes to Talmud and Kaballah.

I find a pen, and I tear off a not-too-stained scrap of the *Tribune*. I ask him to write it down for me.

In the rearview mirror, his head is shaking.

"Ah, you can't write Hebrew?" I say. "Never mind. When I let you off, you repeat it, and I'll jot it down."

For the rest of the journey, we exchange anecdotes about our previous lives. What he got up to with Arafat and Co. About the religious settler movement, and my curious misadventures within it. Each of us seeking to top the other's tale— for that's the rule in this country: Whoever tells the best story wins. . . .

Of course I win. For my stories have everything—they have tragedy; they have glory; they have pathos. They have a hero you can identify with who is also the victim who is myself. They have a beginning, a middle, and an end. I wouldn't be surprised if they turn out to have a moral. And on top of that I assure you they are all true. . . . Whereas his stories, oh, they begin convincingly, they seem plausible and gripping and funny and moving at first, but just as they are about to reach the punch line—my attention is broken: I am distracted by something on the ground or in the air—his stories never conclude. Mind you, the Arab never gives up. I will say that for him. He's persistent as Scheherazade. He talks as much as I do. . . .

Until we have to brake suddenly. One of those checkpoints.

Israeli troops, from the border police. My passenger, myself, and the spleen all have to get out.

Ahmed shows them his ID; they glance at it cursorily.

The spleen is borrowed; and returned with a shudder.

Then they inspect my papers. My identity card. My driver's license. My gun permit.

Suspicious: "What are you? A Jewish extremist?"

"On the contrary."

A soldier pushes his head close to mine. As he speaks he whistles through a gap in his teeth. "When exactly are you planning to assassinate the prime minister?"

They say to Ahmed, "You. You can go now."

And to me: "But you . . . you fit the profile. We're going to take apart your car, and find your hidden bombs."

"But my meat . . ." I stammer.

It could be hours before they release me. (Shocking—some of those left-wingers they allow in the army these days: they like nothing better than to harass us settlers.) And meanwhile, the meat, waiting around in the heat of the day—it could be completely spoiled. . . .

Anger enters me. I scream at the border police. I curse them in Hebrew and Yiddish and Aramaic. I raise my hands on high and implore divine intervention. But the fiercer I become, the more determined the soldiers are to block me. They give as good as they get, wobbling the barrels of their rifles under my nose, and spitting out insults so macho as to be incomprehensible.

Ahmed smiles reassuringly.

"Listen. I'm not too far from my destination. I can walk the rest of the way. And as for your spleen . . . I'll carry it home for you."

"Why thank you! How can I ever repay you?"

I tell him my address. "You can go in the back way. It's never locked. Put the meat in the fridge. . . . If my wife and children see you, just wave hello. . . . You can stay for supper, of course. Stay as long as you want!"

"And about the recipe?"

"Oh. When I get home, you can tell me it."

So I stand at the checkpoint, calm now—while the bored soldiers, with their screwdrivers and chisels, take my VW apart. . . . And I watch the Arab carrying the meat off in his hands. He strides in sandals along the winding black road, between glaring white cliffs, under the sun. His kaffiyeh is pulled over his head, to shade him. I see him follow the road up a slope . . . then down . . . then up again . . . and just as he is about to descend on the final curve into the settlement . . .

There is a mark in the sky—a dot—then the size of a letter—then as vast as whole pages of text. . . . It is an eagle, swooping out of nowhere.

I see it. The soldiers, their hands held to their foreheads as if saluting, see it. But Ahmed, intent on his dripping burden, does not seem to be aware of anything out of the ordinary . . . until the bird sinks its talons into the meat and in one swift sharp tug rips it away. . . . The creature lofts into heaven, carrying the spleen up with it.

The Arab shakes his fist at the eagle.

"You fool!" he cries, his voice echoing across the hills of Samaria, in a language I now at last understand and cannot interrupt. "You fool! You've got the meat, but I, only I have the recipe!"

Did Moshe Dayan Have a Glass Eye?

- If he did, what color?
- If not, why not?
- If a glass eye winks beneath an eyepatch, does anybody see it?
- In the land of the one-eyed, are all blinks winks?

These are some of the questions we will try to answer in this chapter.

⤳

- According to Mrs. Nehama Pforzheimer, who had a mad fling with Dayan in the cockpit of a B-1 in June 1952, he did have a glass eye and it was blue, a piercing blue.
- According to Mrs. Shoshana Simantov, who cuddled next to Dayan in the back row of the Theodor Herzl Memorial

Cinema in Petach Tikva in September of 1947, it was green, as green as the grass that grows in the Galilee in the spring.

- According to Colonel Gideon Maoz, who fought alongside Dayan in the Sinai campaign of 1956, there were no matches so Dayan took out his eyeball—which was absolutely transparent—and, holding it above a stack of love letters and top secret instructions, in practically no time he had made a small fire with which he heated up a pot of delicious Turkish coffee.

Yet others doubt it existed at all.

ﺳ

Did Moshe Dayan have a glass eye, underneath the eyepatch?
- His relatives claim they saw it but once.
- Brown, says one child.
- Gray, says another.
- No, the socket was empty, says a surviving great-nephew.
- He kept a condom in there, says Henry Kissinger, of Washington, D.C.
- Hank Younghusband (erstwhile correspondent with the Associated Press) assures us that Dayan had a miniaturized recording device concealed in his socket.
- Major-General Eitan Benami asserts that Dayan secreted a tiny bomb in there, so that if he were ever captured he could blow himself up, along with his persecutors.
- Yet Dr. Yael Ish-Zahav, the pathologist who performed the autopsy on Dayan, declares in a sworn affidavit that no artificial eye was found on him when he died. The

socket was empty. But could the contents have been removed at the moment of, or just before, or just after, death? Did a team of skilled Mossad agents smuggle away what had been hidden there? Or was the eyeball itself abstracted by an obsessed glass eyeball collector, who to this very day guards it as his pride and joy?

~:

And what can be deduced from careful study of the eyepatch itself?

- Mrs. Henny Margolis, who let Dayan orally pleasure her in 1958, says it was odd being with a man who was wearing an eyepatch. He was not quite naked, you see, so it felt a little rude.

- Mrs. Ruti Rosenblock says she specifically asked Dayan to take off his eyepatch, in the course of their relationship on September 22nd, 1963, but he refused on the grounds that it was so much a part of him that she wouldn't recognize him without it—she would think she was with a different man, and this would make him jealous.

- Mrs. Timna Nissenblatt, on the other hand, claims that Dayan most certainly did take his patch off, at least in August 1949, when he let her wear it across her sex. (Yes but did he have a glass eye underneath? She can't say. That wasn't where she was looking.)

- Mrs. Ketura Fine-Yomtov slept with Dayan every night from March 11th to the 18th, 1959 (she claims). He was madly in love with her, and he told her he would give her anything in the whole world, on condition she never looked underneath his eyepatch.

Naturally on the final night, she did indeed lift the eye-patch, and peek.

She had feared he might be concealing a horrific sight—but on the contrary, his glass eye was exquisitely beautiful. Just then he woke up. "Since you have disobeyed my instructions, you will never see me again." He put on his military uniform, and was borne away in a chauffeur-driven Jeep.

᠁

And was the eyeball buried with him, on the Mount of Olives?

- In 1972 Moshe Dayan was digging for Canaanite sar-cophagi at an archeological site in the vicinity of Jericho, illegally. Professore Etienne Balu, formerly of the Université de Paris, says that the two of them joked that when Dayan's own grave would be looted, thousands of years in the future, everything of him would have rotted apart from his glass eye. "My eye will be in the Israel Museum! Yes!"

- An alternative perspective comes from his physician, Dr. Peretz Rappaport. Dr. Rappaport states that Dayan did indeed possess a glass eye, but he seldom wore it, due to irritation of the underlying tissue. Dr. Rappaport had prescribed an ointment to alleviate this condition.

Notwithstanding (Dr. Rappaport asserts), Moshe Dayan, who was often viewed as a tough manly figure, did in fact suffer pangs like the rest of us, beneath his eyepatch.

- Ms. Bruria Benyishai, a nurse at Israel's most exclusive glass-eyeball clinic, says that Dayan, quite a dandy, came in regularly for eyeball refittings.

"And I wonder which of *your* eyeballs is false?" he would quiz her, flirtatiously.

ܢ

And what about the phenomenon of the so-called "phantom eye"?

There are those who have lost an eye who imagine they still possess it. They suppose they can "see" with it; "squint" with it, and "wink" with it.

"And weep with it?" (our interviewer asks).

"Not beyond the bounds of possibility," concede the relevant authorities.

ܢ

How did he lose the eye in the first place?
- In battle, pierced by shrapnel?
- Or was it rather torn out by a jealous husband?
- Or is it the case that, as a fifteen-year-old lad in Kibbutz Degania Aleph, in love with one-eyed Mrs. Batya Dvash, wife of a cowman, he tore out his own eye to prove his devotion to her; but she scorned him nonetheless; and so he was impelled to become a warrior to show himself worthy.
- Did Golda Meir have a glass eye, but nobody knew?

ܢ

During the Six Day War, Dayan encountered a common soldier, Pvt. Dan Arad, who had lost an eye on the Syrian front but had not yet received an artificial eye, due to the constraints of the bureaucracy of the Israel Defense Forces. *(Have you deposited your original eyeball in the container provided? Yes or No?)* Dayan instantly extracted his own prosthetic eyeball and gave it to Pvt. Arad. "Your need is greater than mine."

- Truth or Myth?

ـﺞ

On the Day of Resurrection, will Moshe Dayan be wearing an eyepatch? And what will he have on beneath it?

- No. Nothing.

Because on that Day, we shall all be remade in our Perfect Bodies.

- But Dayan would not be Dayan without his eyepatch, no?

On the Day of Resurrection, there shall be no Moshe Dayan.

Shaking Hands with Theodor Herzl

⌁ **Although it is November, Jerusalem is hot. There is a** white dust on the hills and alleys and the homburg hat of the notable writer and thinker Dr. Theodor Herzl. His black beard is itching. It is 1898. Two flunkeys in canary-yellow livery lean beside the Byzanto-Romanesque double doors of the Grand Levantine Hotel on Jaffa Road. Herzl enters. The doors swing shut and bang him from behind.

"Ahem," says Herzl. The clerk at the reception desk says, "One minute, sir." The clerk's head is bent over the acrosticon puzzle in the overseas edition of *The Chicago Clarion and Puzzler*. The clerk considers solutions; he angles his skull; his immaculate hair-part teeters like the needle on a weighing machine. "And what can I do for you, sir?" "I have reserved a room. The name is Dr. Herzl." "It is very difficult. We have little space. The German kaiser is paying a state visit to the Pasha so most of our suites are—" "Yes, yes. That in fact is precisely why I myself am in—" "What was the name, sir?" The clerk glances up; he peers at Herzl's nose through pince-nez. "I am afraid we have nothing suitable, Mr. Cohen—" "Dr. Herzl." "Perhaps, on some future occasion, Mr. Levy—" "Dr. Herzl." "Next year, possibly, or in the new century. . . ." "But I insist!" Herzl drums his fist on the counter. "I have come all the way from Vienna to Jerusalem expressly to meet the—!" 7 Down is WAN GERMAN STONE. Herzl flings up an arm in a theatrical gesture. The clerk blinks. Herzl orates, "Do you expect me to sleep in the gutter?!" "That," says the clerk, neatly penciling in PALESTINE, "is entirely your own decision, sir."

Whom should Herzl bump into as he stumbles backward out of the Grand Levantine Hotel but his old chum Siegfried Perl. "Good to see you, Tancred!" says Perl, slapping Herzl on the back. "Tancred?" says Herzl, slapping back. "My name is Dr. Theodor Herzl." "Don't you remember? Vienna University? The Alemanna Club? Your nickname?" "Of course I remember . . . er . . . Galahad. But what are you doing in Palestine?" "I live here. I am a Zionist. Zionism is the name of a political movement headed by a certain Dr. Theodor . . . Surely not?" Herzl blushes and nods. Perl says, "Then you must come round for pastries and coffee! Where are you staying?" "Well, actually . . . " "Then you must stay at my house. No, I insist!"

Perl guides Herzl through the narrow rutted alleys. "I live at 19 Mehmet Ali Street," says Perl. "It is quite easy to find. You just follow the stations of the Via Dolorosa. Here you are flagellated. Here you slip and fall. Just before you are crucified, make a sharp left."

As Herzl follows his friend along the winding route, he smells an odd, nasty but richly nostalgic smell. He cannot quite place it.

Herzl is made welcome at 19 Mehmet Ali Street. He likes the look of the place at once: it has such a reassuringly cluttered Central European air. Here is a brilliant Turkish kilim on the floor; here is another one on the table. Here is the mantelpiece, weighed down with Meissen shepherdesses and Byzantine oil lamps. The walls are hung with lots of little German oil paintings in the Levantine mode: an odalisque leans against a palm tree; a Bedouin warrior sits upright on his camel; a bejeweled sultan decapitates a negro slave. "Which reminds me," says Herzl, "I am to be received by the kaiser tomorrow. I must make a good impression. He has influence with the Ottomans. I will persuade him to favor a Jewish state in Palestine! *If you will it, it is no dream!*" Herzl adds, quoting himself. "Bravo!" says Perl. The other members of Perl's family also express their admiration. Perl introduces them. "Here is my son, Karl-Heinz." A thin, spotty youth, clapping very softly. "And this is my daughter, Brunhilde." An aproned girl with floury fingers; she claps, and the white powder rises in a shaft of sunshine. "And last but not least, my dear lady wife. Her name is—" A dark, plump woman, pearl-earring-ed; she pouts at Herzl. "You may call her Frau Perl."

So Herzl is settled down, in the master bedroom of course. Herr and Frau Perl move temporarily into Brunhilde's room.

Brunhilde is assigned a camp bed in the kitchen. One effect of these maneuverings and shiftings is to displace four chamber pots; these are lined up against a wall of the sitting room. At this point, Karl-Heinz, a shy, serious young man, makes the first and only joke of his life. In years to come, at dinner parties and soirees, he will tell of Herzl's visit and repeat this witticism. Since the pun translates poorly from German into Hebrew, he will have to explain the punch line at length. "Ach," says Karl-Heinz, "This house was so *commode* and now it is full of commodes!"

Coffee and cakes are to be served shortly in the sitting room. Frau Perl grinds the coffee beans in a cylindrical copper device which resembles a land mine. Herzl offers to assist. Frau Perl narrows her eyes at Herzl and says, "Such a gentleman!" Herzl knocks over the grinder and the beans scatter on the floor. Herzl gets down on hands and knees and retrieves them. Frau Perl joins him, crawling alongside, and panting, "Such a gentleman! Such a gentleman!" Herzl and Frau Perl simultaneously grab the same bean; their fingers touch. "The Hegelian synthesis of the nation-state, in re Zionism, is the instantiation of the ethnos, would you not agree, Dr. Herzl?" says Perl, who was sitting on the sofa all along. "Yes," says Herzl, rising to his feet.

Turkish coffee is ground and percolated and poured into the best Rosenthal china coffee cups. Brunhilde enters from the kitchen bearing a silver platter loaded with a massive chocolate cake topped with whipped cream. "Tell me, Dr. Herzl," Brunhilde says, presenting him with a generous slice, "Is my Sachertorte as scrumptious as the Sachertorte at Sacher in Vienna?" Herzl tastes the offering. He chews a mouthful, slowly. In his considered opinion, the cake is overbaked and too sweet. "Certainly, Brunhilde." Throughout Brunhilde's prolonged old age, whenever she has the opportunity to feed her children and grandchildren her favorite dry sugary Sachertorte, she will mutter, "So aristocratic! Such Kultur! As good as in Sacher, he said, better even!" And her family will nod. And she will mumble to herself: "'Delicious, Brunhilde,' he said. 'Mmm, Brunhilde,' he said. 'Yum yum, Brunhilde,' he said. Nobody calls me Brunhilde, now. I have a new Israeli name. I know it begins with B...Bracha?...Beruria?...Bilha? Oh, I'll forget my own name next." Herzl also samples Linztorte and Apfelstrudel. He makes appropriate comments. Everybody is satisfied.

It is bedtime. Herzl is lying on his back between the sheets of the double bed. His neck is pressing on the hard bolster. He is reviewing his tactics for the forthcoming meeting with the kaiser. He is sucking his beard. He blows out the candle. He cannot rest comfortably in this strange bed. He turns on his right side; he smells Perl's male odor. He rolls over onto the other half of the bed; he is disturbed by the faintest hint of Frau Perl's *Nuit d'Amour*. He falls asleep.

An odalisque, leaning against a palm tree, is waving to a tall turbaned Bedouin seated on a cream-colored camel on top of a pile of shiny brown camel droppings. The odalisque, who is Brunhilde, assures Herzl that the droppings are at least as delicious as those made in Vienna. A sultan, waving a bloody sword, commands Herzl to eat the stuff. Delicious, says Herzl compliantly; though in fact it tastes dry and sugary. The Bedouin, who is Perl, informs Herzl that he will have to stay in this position forever to demonstrate his Zionist commitment. The camel licks Herzl's beard; the camel is Frau Perl. The camel caresses Herzl's rib cage with a bony ankle; or the sultan's sword is poking his heart; or the kaiser himself is posing heroically with his jackboot on the recumbent Herzl.

Herzl awakes. He is lying on the very edge of the double bed. Some complex hard object is digging into his side. He rolls over and pulls back the sheets. He was sleeping on Frau Perl's whalebone corset.

It is morning. A harsh sun angles through a gap in the shutter and hits Herzl's head. A muezzin calls all good men to prayer and rouses Herzl. Herzl arranges himself with care. He brushes his hair, beard, teeth, and tailcoat. He fastens his starched collar with a pearl collar stud, and, for double security, holds it in place with a safety pin at the back.

Herzl strolls into the sitting room. Perl greets him with a firm handshake and a cry of "Long live the Zionist ideal!" Herzl says, "Ah, good morning." Frau Perl rises from the sofa; her hair is done up in a chignon and she is wearing a low-cut dress; she looks at Herzl and says nothing. At last, she says, "Did you sleep well?" Herzl considers how to reply. She says, "Isn't that muezzin drone simply awful?" Herzl says, "Very well, thank you. And you?" She says, "My! you look smart." Herzl says, "Yes, quite dreadful." She says, "Would you like a little music?" Herzl says, "You're attractively dressed yourself." "A Jewish state or a state for Jews, that is the question, is it not?" says Perl loudly, "do you want some coffee?" Herzl nods. Perl shouts at the kitchen door, "Karl-Heinz! Make the coffee for my old friend. Brunhilde! Bring on the strudel." Frau Perl repeats, "Would you like a little music?" Perl says, "Surely you're not going to the kaiser without a top hat? He'll have your head chopped off if you don't wear a top hat. Top people are very keen on top hats. Not to worry, I've got a top hat upstairs somewhere, you can borrow mine." Perl goes in search of his top hat. Whenever the name of Herzl will crop up in political discussions in years to come, Perl will always refer to him as "What's-his-name-I-lent-my-top-hat-to."

In contrast, Frau Perl will refuse to mention Herzl. She will say, "Ach, men, always talking this boring politics." Now, she is alone in the sitting room with Herzl. She walks over to a window niche, where there is a high shelf set with Dresden figurines and half a Philistine saucer. Underneath it is Frau Perl's prize possession: the symphonion: a cross between a pianola and a phonograph. Frau Perl turns the handle to crank the machine. She selects a shiny metal disk pierced with slots in a spiral pattern. She places it on the turntable. The symphonion emits a tinny music-box sound; it is playing the beginning of the overture to *Tannhäuser*. Frau Perl turns to face Herzl. She says, "Ah, music, it is my soul!" She walks towards him. "There is little good music in Jerusalem. How I miss it. My husband doesn't like music. Have you been to the latest Strauss in Vienna?" "No," says Herzl. "How I envy you! We must talk about music in the twilight." "I won't be here this evening. After meeting the kaiser, I will catch the train to Haifa, and then the ship. Thank you for your kind hospitality." "Farewell!" Frau Perl opens her arms wide to embrace Herzl and bursts into tears.

At this point, Karl-Heinz and Brunhilde enter from the kitchen bearing a jug of coffee and a plate of strudel smothered in whipped cream, and Perl comes down the stairs carrying a large candy-striped box that he opens to reveal a dusty, slightly moth-eaten top hat. Herzl smells four smells: the aroma of coffee, the odor of strudel, the stink of mothballs, and *Nuit D'Amour*. Herzl will shortly be received by the kaiser who will listen to his plea for a Jewish National Home in Palestine and turn the request down flat. And Herzl will deliver a speech at the World Zionist Congress in which he will argue that there is nothing special about Palestine and why should the Jews not settle in, oh, say, Uganda.

Now Herzl sees the four members of the Perl family advancing on him from every direction. Suddenly, he recognizes that strange nostalgic stench which had troubled him earlier. It is the Jewish Smell. He backs toward the door. "Go away!" he cries. "Go away, you Jews!"

A Tooth for a Tooth

⌒ **I had been sent there. I was in Jerusalem, at the behest of** a couple of news magazines, during the late summer and early fall of 1993, covering the Israel–PLO story—faxing back copy on each sub-story as it broke, each factoid, each indication of peace or no-peace. I (along with myriads of other reporters from around the world) was at Damascus Gate on that extraordinary afternoon when Palestinian youths finally clambered up it, on top of it, as high as the ramparts, and waved their outsized flag—a homemade flag, stitched together by Auntie Fatma on her prized electric Singer. Afterwards the shabab tried to transport it in a procession through the Gate: it proved too tall to fit upright in the Old City, and had to be borne at shoulder height like a coffin—and the Israeli police were turning a blind eye throughout.

I was in the TV lounge of the American Colony Hotel (I and a score of my fellow reporters) clinking our glasses of grape-fruit juice and cheering the historic Rabin–Arafat handshake as it happened. Bliss, it seemed, in that TV-glow to be alive, and to be a foreign correspondent was very heaven. Jerusalem then was thronged with every journalist in the world, apparently, as if on a Day of Resurrection; so-and-so was forever bumping into what's-his-name he had last crossed paths with in London or New York or Mogadishu or Sarajevo. . . . And all the while my canines were aching.

I tried not to think about it, of course. I had work to do. The distraction was what I couldn't afford: I refused to admit any weakness. For over a week I managed to convince myself that I felt no pain, or that if I did it was a twinge, something that would pass. But ultimately I had no choice: nobody can ignore bodily suffering forever.

It was an Israeli friend of mine, a poet, who saw through my self-deception. We were meeting in the lobby of the used-to-be-the-Hilton Hotel (she was supposed to be introducing me to a contact in military intelligence, a pal of hers from her tank corps days, who never showed), and instead of smiling at her in greeting, I winced. She said, "Is life so bad?" I confessed. She unhesitatingly recommended Dr. Peretz ("Fritz") Kahn. He had had a most triumphant career, one of the leading dentists of his generation, she said, and although he was now officially retired he was nevertheless willing to take on a few personally recommended clients at a modest charge, just to keep his hand in. As a matter of fact he had been responsible for her own incisor-capping and her root canal work—and look how attractively she laughed.

And so, within an hour I was in the plush neighborhood of
Old Katamon pushing open the olivewood gate and walking up
the path that leads to Dr. Kahn's house. The garden was a paradise. There were rows of trees—trees from every continent:
date palm, gingko, sugar maple, monkey puzzle, Japanese
cherry that would blossom so prettily in a different season. . . .
There were innumerable varieties of plants and embedded vegetables—each, to my eye then, resembling a different kind of
extractable green tooth. . . . And that pale dust which is everywhere in Jerusalem, being eroded from the limestone on which
the city is built, was drifting through shafts of sunshine, and
sugaring the bark and foliage and my own skin. . . . All I wanted
was to have my hurt taken away.

Which was happening, or at least beginning to happen, a
minute later. Kahn hadn't actually operated on me; he hadn't
prodded my teeth and gums yet; not so much as peered inside;
but something about his manner, his very presence, was having
a soothing effect (the mystery was not to be analyzed, I considered, else it would vanish). I was reclining in his dentist's chair,
a pre-War model upholstered in red leather, in the middle of an
overfurnished living room, while this old man with a come-
dian's face, this Kahn, paced around me in his floppy slippers.
"Aaah," I said. He tugged and twisted and trembled a ring from
his middle finger with the grace of a conjurer plucking an ace
from thin air; the ring was gold and headed with a Roman coin.
Kahn set it down on a fringed velvet shawl draped over the
upright piano. Beside the ring were several framed snapshots of
babies and children; also an ancient earthenware oil lamp and

dish, museum pieces: millennia old and unbroken. He washed his hands. I stared straight ahead. I noted a black-and-white wedding photograph on the wall in front of me: the groom was Kahn, a young man then. Also, next to it, another wedding photograph, in color, with a middle-aged Kahn playing the same role, kissing a different bride. He touched my jaw with his dry, faintly soap-smelling fingertips. He entered my mouth with investigatory speculum and pick.

And meanwhile we conversed. He began by quizzing me about my job. For obvious reasons the dialogue was an unequal one: his questions were much longer and more coherent than my answers. In the brief gaps in his work—while he was switching instruments or changing his grip—I managed to blurt, in a pidgin of English and Hebrew, some makeshift explanations and justifications of the role of the free press in a democracy, and what I reckoned were the chances for a lasting peace. . . . I shouldn't suppose any of my comments were particularly original or noteworthy. I distinctly remember uttering, in a deprecatory, even mocking tone, the word "revenge" (actually I used the Hebrew word for it, which, having so many Biblical associations—"Vengeance is mine, saith the Lord"—can't really be translated), and Kahn sighed and said he could tell me about revenge. A blurry closeup of his white-haired knuckles drifted across my vision.

Something complicated ensued—to do with taking X-rays of my jaw. I wasn't allowed to move let alone speak for several minutes. I concentrated on my role as subject. . . . I realized the old man was in full spate, telling a story about dentistry in the early years of the State of Israel.

"It was about 1950," he was saying. "All kinds of exotic Jews were immigrating into the land. There were mountain dwellers from the Caucasus, in their gorgeous embroideries, and . . . perhaps you have heard of Operation Magic Carpet, when the Yemenite Jews were flown here 'on eagle's wings' as they say? I worked in the free clinic, checking the teeth of the new arrivals; most of them had surprisingly good dentition, considering their poor diet. For example I remember a Tunisian grandmother with her teeth painted black for beauty's sake; nevertheless there was nothing amiss, odontologically speaking. Also a family of newcomers from the Crimea who insisted on gold fillings, although they all had complete sets of false teeth already; it turned out there was a black market in . . . but that is another story.

"And you must remember, Mr. T___, that those were dangerous years. People forget. Young people never knew. They read in their history books there was a war in '47 and another war in '56 and they think that in between we lived in peace. Peace! Every day in the newspapers there was another terrorist raid from across the Jordan, or an incident at the Egyptian frontier. . . . Kidnap. Murder. Rape. . . . Ach, Mr. T___, but you don't want me to talk about politics. . . ."

"No," I said. "I don't."

"You moved your head! Like I told you not to. Now I will have to take the X-ray all over again.

"Now one day in 1951 . . . no, it must have been 1952 . . . I had just begun establishing my reputation in reconstructive and cosmetic dentistry, and had moved into this house. Naturally I was only taking patients who could pay out of their own pocket, and I was no longer providing a service for the immigrants—the door opened from my waiting room and an entire family of Moroccan Jews shuffled in. I could tell they were Moroccan, from some village in the Atlas mountains, because the old woman had on a headdress with coins and shells around it, which is typical of that region. Of course the men were wearing just the frayed trousers and shirts that all the Sephardim used to have then. . . . How could I turn them away? 'Come in,' I said to them. 'Come in, friends, and tell me your dental problems.'

"They stood by the door. They didn't move or reply. Obviously they didn't understand Hebrew. Well I know a little Arabic (I lived in the Old City during the Mandate; how could I not?) so I repeated the request in that language. However they didn't budge. One of the men stammered a phrase which I couldn't make out. Of course my Arabic is the Palestinian dialect, and their Maghrebi kind is very different. . . . Fortunately they had brought along a boy of eleven or twelve, who spoke Hebrew and served as the translator.

"The boy explained. It was his Uncle Yom Tov—a stocky man about twenty, with a sullen expression and a bruise on his chin, standing close to the wall—who needed treatment. I beckoned the man over. I gestured that he should sit down and relax, just where you are sitting now, Mr. T___. I told the boy to assure his uncle that there would be no pain.

"'What's the matter?' I asked the boy, and the boy asked the man. The man mumbled a few syllables which the boy translated: 'Nothing.' So I said, 'Nothing?' thinking it was a case of scaredness (they often are scared, you know, but I always tell them it's much better to know the truth, what has to be done— and then I administer an anesthetic, and afterwards the rotten root is pulled out and the suffering has vanished and we can all forget about it), 'don't worry, Yom Tov, I won't hurt you, I use the latest techniques.' And the boy spoke to his uncle, and the matriarch was making a sign against the Evil Eye, and meanwhile I was sterilizing my instruments.

"'Open your mouth wider!' ... No, not you, Mr. T___, yours is already as wide as it needs to be—that's what I told the boy to tell Yom Tov. 'I won't bite you,' I joked. And eventually, reluctantly—the man let me examine him.

"His teeth were perfect! I have seldom seen teeth in such immaculate condition. Better than yours, Mr. T___, you're not brushing properly in the corners; and remind me to give you some simple advice on flossing before you go. . . . You know it is their custom to chew on a certain kind of twig to clean their teeth, which is really a very effective method. . . .

"The boy said: 'Uncle Yom Tov wants you to pull out two teeth.'

"I said, 'No. No tooth-pulling needs to be done.'

"The boy repeated the statement.

"And I said it was unnecessary. . . .

"Then the patient spoke, which the boy translated, making the demand for the third time. And for the third time I told him no. . . . And when I looked up the family were standing close around me—they must have tiptoed in while I'd been working—staring into my face and breathing heavily. . . .

"Ah, you must understand, Mr. T___, these Oriental Jews, they have a different culture from us. Of course the Moroccans in question, they were all newcomers, you have to make allowances, they had not learned our customs yet, our mind-set, our *Weltanschauung.* . . .

"And the old woman herself, she pleaded with me, at length,

cajolingly, bitterly; all those coins and shells on her headdress and the fretted silver amulet around her neck and the silvery loops dangling from her ears jangled as she orated...and if I understood little of her rhetoric, I understood the gist of it: 'Do what my son wants. Take out what he wants taken out. Call yourself a Jew and you won't fulfill a simple request? Have mercy!'

"At last she ran out of words, and I addressed the boy: 'You're an Israeli. You'll soon be barmitzvah. You're practically a mensch, insh'allah, already. You speak my language. Tell me: what do the old people really want?'"

Humming to himself *Eine Kleine Nachtmusik*, the dentist removed the X-ray film from my mouth and carried it over to the developing machine, which stood in a mihrab-like niche in the corner of the room. My jaw ached from having been held open so long; I made chewing motions to ease the muscles.

It was strange for me to observe a dentist perform a variety of menial tasks for himself. I am used to the (excuse the stereotyping, but it is what I have encountered) male middle-aged dentist accompanied by a young pretty female helper whose tasks appear to consist of handing her boss things, upping the theatricality, and giving him a sense of his own importance—a kind of conjurer's assistant. But Kahn was his own assistant: he was both master and servant, both star and walk-on part, perhaps both male and female as well—for he possessed a touch of that androgyny that surfaces in some old men...his plump pale jowls, his fussiness.

While I had been thinking these thoughts Kahn had been continuing his story. I had not been paying attention, really—but it was easy enough to fill in the gap. In short: the patient,

Yom Tov, had been involved in a fight the previous evening with a man from another Jewish family hailing from the same village (Kahn used the Yiddish word *landsman*) and had knocked out a couple of his enemy's front teeth. According to their custom, his rival was entitled to claim Yom Tov's teeth by way of compensation.

I asked, "What was the fight about?"

"Money? A woman? Often these youths fight about nothing at all. What does it matter?"

"You mean, Yom Tov had to be punished?"

"No. No, it had nothing to do with 'punishment'—as we use the term. Perhaps Yom Tov behaved badly and perhaps he didn't. Perhaps his opponent was drunk and picked a fight, then tripped over his own feet and knocked his teeth out on the pavement. The point is: the one man had suffered and so the other had to suffer also, for the sake of symmetry."

Kahn considered an array of bright, sharp instruments in a padded red velvet case. He made his selection.

"And did you?" I said. "Did you agree to extract the teeth?"

Kahn sighed. "I am not a religious man, but I hold there to be important moral values in our traditional teaching." He pointed at the Prayer for the Healer by Maimonides (a kind of Jewish version of the Hippocratic Oath), which was framed in ebony over the mantelpiece. "And since they were religious, naturally I spoke to them in a way they would, or should, understand.

"Open your mouth wide again, Mr. T___.

"You know where it says in the Torah: An eye for an eye, a tooth for a tooth?. . . " (He intoned the quote twice, first in Hebrew then in English. I nodded.) ". . . Well that King James version is a deliberate mistranslation, in fact it is a slander, a blood-libel! Christians pretend that Jews are vengeful, they pretend it means that if I knock out your organ you should knock out mine, but if you read it in context, in Exodus where it comes from, you'll see it says nothing of the kind! The Torah states that if I injure you then I owe you financial compensation, and the meaning is that if I damage your eye I should pay an appropriate amount to make up for your loss of vision, if it's your tooth I harm then I should compensate you for your difficulty in eating—for each crime the exact punishment—not revenge but justice!

"What I said to you I said to them. All this. To the Moroccans. And the boy translated it on my behalf. This and much more. I told them the midrash about how God was so merciful that even while Pharaoh and his host were drowning in the Red Sea . . . Ah, to them I spoke in their language and to you I will speak in ours. Mr. T___: revenge is not a word that should belong in our vocabulary."

It felt as if Kahn were digging into my teeth and gums, mining them, seeking ore. Hurtless yet thorough. A series of internal thuds and explorations. The filling in my molar due to too much candy in my early teens; the bridgework necessitated by my having fallen off the pillion seat of a fortunately slow-moving Harley, aged twenty, not wholly sober. Kahn was investigating all these, and more, appraising my dental history.

He removed his instruments from my mouth temporarily while he sought a differently tipped probe. The set of tools off to my left glittered like the reflections off a liquid. He touched them lightly, as if he were dabbling his fingertips in a meniscus.

"So you refused?" I asked.

Kahn reentered my mouth. "Ach, what could I do? The boy told me: if I didn't perform the operation, then the victim, or a member of his family, would have the right to knock out two of the perpetrator's teeth, by brute force. This is their law. Their Levantine notion of . . . " (he said the English words in a parodic British accent) ". . . fair play.

"Yom Tov mimed punching his own mouth, to make sure I understood.

"I put the patient under total anesthetic—we used ether in those days; I think I got a whiff of it myself: I remember feeling an absurd desire to sleep, an absurder desire to laugh. . . . And I extracted a pair of wisdom teeth. . . . I justified it to myself . . . " (in fact Kahn used a biblical idiom that is current in modern Hebrew; literally: "I said in my heart") ". . . often wisdom teeth act up and cause pain later in one's life, so possibly I was doing him a favor—prophylactically speaking."

His probe scraped my gum. I suppressed an exclamation. He delicately shifted his instrument.

Kahn reminisced, "Oh those wisdom teeth were big, and deeply embedded. They came out all bloody, with twisted roots. . . . I didn't hurt you just now, Mr. T___, did I? Good . . . I stuffed cotton wool soaked in clove essence in the gums, which was how we treated the after-pain in the early 1950s.

"The boy had his palms held out. He wanted the teeth.

"So I gave him them. And he held them very close under his nose, and inspected them in detail. Then the boy handed them to a man (his older brother, I think), who examined them and passed them on to somebody else . . . and in due course the whole family had a good look, and they ended up with the old woman. It was like—you know how it is among religious people, on Saturday nights, at the end of Shabbat, they take the sweet-smelling *besamim* in its pierced silver holder, and pass it around so everybody can take a sniff, to revive them spiritually, to reconcile them to the profane working week—well that's what it looked like. And the matriarch, she gave the pair of wisdom teeth back to the boy to hold, as if it were his plaything, his toy. . . .

"No, not a toy! He held the teeth in his clenched right fist with pride; they were the badge of his office, his scepter . . . which was just, since, by virtue of knowing Hebrew, he had become their de facto leader, their boy-king.

"The king thanked me on behalf of his people. His manner was strangely mature. His Hebrew was formal and curt. He stated that I deserved a reward on heaven and on earth. The old woman set about thumbing through a bunch of paper money she kept rolled in a fold of her many-layered skirt. . . . But I told her and him and the entire family, 'No. Please. No.' (God forbid I should take payment for a useless operation, an unethical one in fact—and I began to regret what I had done.) I said, 'Give it to charity, instead. Give it to the poor, the sick, widows and orphans. . . .'

"The patient was still in his chair, groggy from the anesthetic, staring into space. I chucked his cheek, I patted him on the shoulder, and I said, slowly, in simple Hebrew, simple Arabic: 'It is over, Yom Tov. The operation is over now. The suffering is over. . . .'

"And he gave a horrible grin. And I thought: maybe he misunderstood? Then I thought: my teeth removal has changed the shape of his mouth, his jawline, his whole face, forever, and for the worse.

"And the man, Yom Tov, he muttered something—as he struggled up from his chair. And by the way you too are free to put on your coat, Mr. T___. I won't be a minute."

I stayed put.

"Then the boy shook my hand. He thanked me once more. He explained that the family had to leave now so as to pay a call on Doctor—"

Kahn wrinkled up his features, making an ugly face, and spat, hygienically, into the basin intended for that purpose, beside the armrest of the chair.

I asked: "What doctor? What was his name? Was there something bad about him?"

Kahn echoed: "Was there something bad about him! He was a surgeon. Killed in the Suez Campaign, may his soul find some kind of peace. 'Bad?' Not bad: he was competent. Yes: 'bad.' He had a reputation, he was unethical, he performed . . . you know, "operations"—any kind of operations, anything, anything for money! I hated to think . . . If I am to be honest, Mr. T___, this is what upset me: I hated to think I was associated in anybody's mind with such a person."

"I don't understand. Did Yom Tov have some injury? Why would they need a surgeon?"

"Exactly what I asked the family, Mr. T___! 'But why?' I said. 'I have already performed the extraction. The task is complete. Just as you requested. All is fine. All is finished. In an efficient and professional manner. All is, as you say, "revenged." Why do you need to take Yom Tov to Doctor . . . to this man? What can he do for you that I have not done already?'

"Yom Tov said nothing; he shrugged. The boy said nothing. The family was silent; still.

"At last they all nodded and bowed at me; the matriarch thanked me politely; she was squeezing her amulet.

"Yom Tov had succeeded in rising from the chair. He hadn't yet gotten over the anesthetic, not properly. He was swaying like a man waist-deep in a stream. The boy gave him back his own blood-stained wisdom teeth. Which Yom Tov clutched in front of him, between finger and thumb—like one of those Christian saints who display a severed body part, showing the nature of their martyrdom."

Kahn held up the X-ray negatives to the light, gripping them by the edges to avoid fingerprints. He didn't stop talking.

"I can't get over how happy Yom Tov looked . . . I don't mean happy: he wasn't; I mean, oh, satisfied: no he wasn't that either: he still craved more. . . . He wanted revenge so badly—against himself, since there wasn't anybody else to blame.

"The family exited. It was a procession: the matriarch waddling majestically at the front, Yom Tov and the boy taking up the rear. And as they opened that door there—through which you entered, Mr. T___, and which you're going to go out through shortly—I saw, beyond them, clustered in the waiting room, another family. A similar family; almost a mirror image in fact; from their clothes and demeanor these people too were immigrants from the same region of Morocco. Likewise a matriarch wearing a headdress with gold coins around it. Likewise staring, rather embarrassed men of varied ages. Likewise a boy to serve as translator, if need be. Likewise a man of about Yom Tov's age and build. Yom Tov handed his own wisdom teeth over to this man—who glanced at them, grunted, and pocketed them."

I asked: "This other man, was he—"

"Yes. It must have been quite a fight. The defeated rival, two of his incisors were missing; there were scratches on his nose and cheek; and a stained bandage covered his left eye socket."

Kahn slid his Roman ring back onto its finger.

"And as for you, Mr. T___, I wish you all the best in your journalism, in whichever of the world's trouble spots you are sent to next."

"But what about my—"

"I can find no decay in your canines. Your dentition is entirely adequate."

"But I assure you, Dr. Kahn, I definitely—"

"You'd be surprised how often patients come to me with their pains, and it turns out there is nothing the matter with them, nothing wrong, nothing in the teeth, that is."

Arafat's Elephant

⌁ I was invited to the home of Mr. Al-Hanani (not his real
name, of course), head of one of the most distinguished families
of Nablus. His villa is located a dozen kilometers from the
urban center, at the end of a winding road; no doubt once—
before the city enlarged in girth and height—it commanded a
magnificent view.

Mr. Al-Hanani himself greeted me at the door. He spoke
excellent English, with an Oxford accent. We asked after the
health of one another's families. I removed my shoes. He took
me by the arm and led me along a corridor into a drawing
room. He gestured that I should sit next to him, on a divan covered with an antique Turkish rug. I noted various elaborately
chased silver vessels, disposed on low tables; higher up were
photographs of my host in the company of notables. From time

to time his sons ventured into the room to peek at us. His wife, elegant in a long dress and headscarf, appeared only briefly when she brought us a tray of mint tea served in delicate, ruby-tinted gold-rimmed glasses, along with a dish of sweetmeats.

For a minute or so we sat in companionable silence. He stared at a cabinet, of a dark wood inlaid with mother-of-pearl, situated directly opposite us: its doors were open to reveal a television tuned to a news station—the sound was off, and interference fuzzed the monochrome image. He sighed, and then he discussed a certain recent proposal to establish a "science park" on the outskirts of Nablus, ostensibly to encourage local high-tech industries. Mr. Al-Hanani expressed doubt this would be of benefit to ordinary Palestinians. To be quite frank, he declared, speaking close to my ear, he suspected it was a scheme that would serve the interest only of certain influential business-men, cronies of . . . Just then a truck carrying building materials to a nearby site drove close by the villa, and its clamor drowned out the rest of my host's comments. . . . From a box decorated with seashells he tugged a single Kleenex, set it on the palm of his right hand, and placed some snacks thereon, proffering them. Would I care for baklava? Would I care for Cadbury's Chocolate Digestive Biscuits?

I would.

And then he told me a story about his ancestors.

"You know, my family has always been here. We are here now. We were here under the Israelis. We were here under the British. We were here in the days of the Ottoman Empire. And we were a remarkable family—nowadays we are what we are—

but once we were renowned for our generosity, our piety, our learning, our wealth—oh yes, we were quite wealthy back then. So remarkable were we that our reputation came to the ear of the sultan himself, in Istanbul (or Constantinople—call it what you wish). Now this particular sultan (whose name escapes me; it really does not matter) who lived back then (a hundred years ago? a thousand?—let us just say: a long time ago) did not approve of anyone anywhere in his empire being wealthy apart from himself. Possibly he feared a rival source of power would develop; possible he was jealous. At any rate, he determined to humble my family. So he summoned the head of the family—my noble ancestor—accompanied by his six sons, to the sultanic court.

"After a long and trying journey, they arrived there, in the palace at the heart of the empire. They presented their letter of invitation; they were ushered into the sultan's presence: they made obeisances and offered appropriate tributes. Whereupon the sultan made an announcement. He was delighted to present my ancestor with a token of his appreciation. My ancestor was to be given an elephant, as a parting gift.

"My ancestor and his sons took charge of the beast—a splendid specimen, imported from India. Naturally they bribed the sultan's head elephant keeper to give them a rapid course of lessons in elephant care. And then, having been dismissed from the court, they returned home, as the sultan had commanded them, taking extreme precautions to safeguard the elephant.

"For (and this was the sultan's scheme) not only is an elephant expensive and awkward to look after, but also, should any serious mishap befall the animal, the family would suffer dire punishment.

"Now, I shall not tell you about the long journey overland from Istanbul to Nablus, and the many adventures that befell my ancestor, his sons, and the elephant. How several times they all came close to death. How once the elephant ran amok in an apple orchard. How once it ran amok in an apricot orchard. How twice it ran amok in a rhubarb patch. How in Antakya it made friends with a dove. How it spied a whale by the Bosporus, and it was in a sulk for seven days. How its usual diet was straw and turnips. How the elephant almost froze crossing the mountains of Lebanon, and my ancestor and his six sons had to sleep close by it, wrapping their limbs about it, warming it with their own bodies. How the sons tried to sell the dung as fertilizer, but bandits kept stealing it. How once near Aleppo ignorant peasants thought the elephant was a devil and shot at it with arrows, which bounced off its thick hide, and then the peasants surrounded it with fire—it burst through the flames, trumpeting loudly—and it made for a mosque where (as it had been trained in Istanbul) it washed its hands and feet, like any good Muslim: it entered and kneeled and lowered its trunk in the direction of Mecca—the ignorant peasants prostrated themselves before the elephant. How it suffered from wind in Tyre. How it accidentally trampled a field of sesame on the outskirts of Nazareth, and my ancestor had to pay extortionate compensation. . . .

"No, you need not know about these and many more adventures. Suffice it to say: the beast arrived safely home in Nablus. It was housed out there—beyond the French windows—where now you can see apartment buildings and an earthmoving machine—all that land used to belong to my family; there were stables and a paddock for our steeds . . . I do apologize for the dust and noise . . . we had an ornamental garden also; our roses were unparalleled throughout the Levant . . . And so, as I was saying, the elephant resided there, and it was excellently cared for, by my ancestor and his six sons and our servants, and for many a long year it was in the best of health until . . . another Chocolate Digestive? . . . it sickened and died.

"Why exactly it passed away I could not tell you. It was rumored that a spell had been cast upon it; or that it had been poisoned by emissaries of a rival family, the . . . best not to name them—they still live below us, in their villa next to the cement works. . . . But I make no accusation: the elephant had been kept under lock and key, groomed only by our most trustworthy servants. Maybe it died of homesickness, being so far from its birthplace? Or from lovesickness, since there was no elephant of the opposite sex for it to mate with?

"Suffice it to say: we had a problem. A very big problem— as big as an . . . *ahem* . . . All the servants who knew of the creature's demise were sworn to secrecy: should they so much as hint that the sultan's gift was not in perfect health, they would pay for their indiscretion with their own lives. In the dead of the night, my ancestor and his sons stripped the skin off the corpse and hung it up to dry. The bones and flesh were buried under the poppy field, there, where the extruded plastic factory is now. . . . Then, a few weeks later, on the occasion of an important religious festival—the Eid al-Fitr—my wise and cunning ancestor announced that he would show the citizens of Nablus what it was that the sultan had presented him with. The common people gathered at the foot of the field, on the edge of our estate. Men came with their wives and their children. The stable doors were opened, and out tottered a large dark animal with a long nose. The onlookers muttered amongst themselves; they clutched their amulets and clicked their beads. *Elephant*, they gasped, *this must be the notorious elephant.* . . . And so it was assured that the message would disseminate, all the way to Istanbul, that the sultan's elephant was doing just fine in the home of my ancestor.

"Actually it was a large bull, with a rolled-up rug strapped to its snout. The people of Nablus had never seen an elephant before, you understand—anything massive with some sort of trunk was enough to convince them.

"So it went on, through the years. Twice a year, on the Eids, my ancestor would display his mock-elephant to the masses. The crowd would ooh and aah; roving entertainers would juggle balls and swallow fire and charm snakes; vendors would sell falafel and cures for impotence; preachers and circumcisers would work the crowd . . . the elephant itself soon became yesterday's news—it remained a convenient focus for the party, however.

"But then, one fine spring, the proclamation reached Nablus. The sultan himself was coming to Palestine! He had decided to go on a pilgrimage to Jerusalem—to the mosque of El-Aksa, to the site from where al-Burak, the Prophet's horse, had taken off heavenward—and it was intended that he should travel by way of our hometown. Surely he would want to behold his elephant. Surely he and his entourage could not be fooled by any dressed-up bull.

"What could we do? We could hardly confess to the sultan that his elephant had passed away. He would torture us for our betrayal, snapping our bones like . . . Another Digestive Biscuit?

Or do try kanafiya: it's the local speciality? . . . And then he'd behead us all, and confiscate our estate.

"My ancestor prayed and mused. He turned over possible plans in his head. He prayed to the Almighty for assistance.

"The sultan was invited into this very house. He sat where you are sitting, on the divan, and he drank tea and ate sweetmeats, just as you are doing now. . . . And then, in the hour before dusk when, as it is written, 'one can scarcely tell black from white,' my ancestor stood beside the sultan, over there, where the television is—and the two of them gazed through what is now the French windows across what used to be the verandah and what is now the building site as far as the stables. . . .

"The stable door opened, as if of its own accord . . . And out it swayed! Yes, the massive creature with the four thick delicate feet, the long strong trunk, the tail, the flapping ears and tiny eyes. What could this be but the original elephant!?

"You see, my wise ancestor had preserved the hide. He had fastened it over a wicker frame, and his six sons were within it—one son to walk inside each leg, plus the eldest son to manipulate the trunk and ears, and the littlest son had the job of whisking the tail.

"The elephant went for quite a stroll—around the rose garden, behind the poppy field, winding in and out between the olive trees . . . never getting too close to the house, of course, lest the sultan should notice something awry.

"The sultan applauded. He thanked my ancestor for his devotion in having guarded the elephant through so many years, solely in order to provide a diversion and spectacle for the

sultan himself, on this one happy occasion. Whereupon...
please feel free to wipe your fingers on a Kleenex... the sultan
took out his Gatling gun and—*ratatatatata!*—shot the elephant
through. Naturally my ancestor had to congratulate the sultan
on his magnificent display of sportsmanship—even though his
six sons lay dying within the tanned hide.

"There is a glass of tea left in the pot. As your host, I am
privileged to offer it to you.... About the elephant, there is little else to say.... Subsequently my ancestor fathered one more
son—a weakling, inferior in every way to his six saintly brothers. It is the last brother, of course, the one who did not make
the long burdensome pilgrimage to Istanbul, and bring home
the elephant, and die as a noble martyr inside it—it is from him
that I and my family descend."

Acknowledgments

╰┈➤ The author would like to thank the many individuals who have assisted in the writing of this work, including Lisa Bernstein, Jonny Geller, Alon Harel, Elizabeth Hollander, Samia Maneh, Batyah Million, Emma Parry, Dawn Seferian, Frank Stewart, Rachel Stroumsa, and others who wish to remain anonymous. The author is grateful also to the Blue Mountain Center, the Djerassi Foundation, the Virginia Center for the Creative Arts, the Corporation of Yaddo, the Ledig Foundation, the Cité des Artes, the Château de Lavigny, and the Rockefeller Center at Bellagio.